Nick Kennedy was spec[illegible] Sammy thought.

Broad shoulders, beautiful biceps, enough hair on his chest to be sexy without him looking like a total gorilla and a definite six-pack.

Mr. December was going to be the best page on the calendar. He could probably sell the calendar all by himself.

But now he'd said there was no wife or girlfriend, she couldn't help wondering: How come a gorgeous man with a good brain and kind eyes was single? Was it because he was a workaholic and his girlfriends tended to get fed up waiting for him to notice them? Or had she missed some major personality flaw?

"What?" he asked, clearly noting that she was staring at him.

"Nothing," she said, embarrassed to discover that her voice was slightly croaky. She really had to get a grip.

The last thing she needed was for her skittish model to work out that she was attracted to him.

But a girl could dream...

Dear Reader,

When I wrote *It Started at a Wedding*, Claire and Ashleigh's best friend politely informed me that she'd rather like her own story, please.

So there I have my go-getting photographer Sammy (who shares my love of architecture and the sea). What drives her to work so hard, and why does she avoid relationships? And, more to the point, who could make her change her mind?

Enter Nick, my barrister with a real sense of responsibility to family—and who's been hurt enough not to want to take risks with relationships.

And getting them together...now, that was a lot of fun. I very much enjoyed the film *Calendar Girls* (and it's close to my heart as my mum died from cancer)—but what if the photographer of a charity calendar was female and fell for one of the models? Especially if he was really straitlaced? And what if she had a big secret as to why she was supporting the charity calendar? That was the perfect start to the story...

Add Christmas (because I just *love* the lights of London at Christmas), some of my favorite bits of the capital, a bit of stubbornness on both sides and a proposal to melt even the most stubborn of hearts...and I hope you enjoy Sammy and Nick's story.

With love,

Kate Hardy

Falling for Mr. December

Kate Hardy

Recycling programs for this product may not exist in your area.

ISBN-13: 978-0-373-74357-5

Falling for Mr. December

First North American Publication 2015

This edition published by arrangement with Harlequin Books S.A.

For questions and comments about the quality of this book, please contact us at CustomerService@Harlequin.com.

Printed in U.S.A.

Award-winning author **Kate Hardy** lives in Norwich, England, with her husband, two children, one spaniel and too many books to count! She's a fan of the theater, ballroom dancing, posh chocolate and anything Italian. She's a history and science geek, plays the guitar and piano, and makes great cookies (which is why she also has to go to the gym five days a week...)

Books by Kate Hardy

HARLEQUIN ROMANCE

Once a Playboy...
Ballroom to Bride and Groom
Bound by a Baby
Behind the Film Star's Smile
Crown Prince, Pregnant Bride
A New Year Marriage Proposal
It Started at a Wedding...

Visit the Author Profile page
at Harlequin.com for more titles.

To Fi, my best friend, with much love.

CHAPTER ONE

SAMMY LAUGHED AS the penny finally dropped. 'So you want me to photograph naked men for you?'

Ayesha, who chaired the Friends of the London Victoria Hospital, squirmed and stared into her latte. 'Put like that, it sounds terrible!'

'I know what you meant. Do it *artistically*,' Sammy said, still smiling. 'A calendar of hot men to raise funds for the cancer ward. It's a great idea. So do you have a bunch of sexy doctors lined up to pose for me?'

'A couple,' Mari, the vice-chair, said. 'But we were thinking maybe we can include other people who've been involved with the ward.'

'Cured patients, so you can say that this is what a cancer survivor looks like? That could work well.' And, for a cause like that, Sammy would seriously think about going public and baring her own leg, if they couldn't get enough models.

'We were thinking relatives of patients,' Ayesha said. 'Ones with high profiles locally. We've got an actor, a musician, a chef, a gardener…'

'So I could maybe shoot them in their own locations, doing their job. That'd work really well,' Sammy said. 'And they're all happy about posing naked—provided I preserve their modesty?'

'Ye—es,' Ayesha said.

The hesitation told her everything. 'You didn't actually tell them it meant posing naked, did you?' Sammy asked.

'We're going to,' Mari said. 'We can talk them into it.'

'As I'll need signed model release forms before I can let you use the photographs, I'm afraid you'll have to do that.' Sammy looked at her diary. 'If you're using the hospital as a location, I could shoot the whole lot in a day, but if I need to go to different places then I'll have to work out a schedule based on the locations and the availability of the models.' She scribbled some notes down on a pad. 'These are the best times for me to do it, but I can also work round a couple of other things if you need me to. Talk to your models and let me know where and when you want me to do the shoots.'

'Sammy, you're a star. Thank you so much,' Ayesha said.

Sammy shrugged off the praise. 'It's the least I can do. If it wasn't for the treatment I had here when I was a teen—' and again two years ago '—then I wouldn't be here. And this means I can give something back.' She smiled. 'This is going to be fun. And we're going to raise a ton of money for the ward.'

Nick folded his arms and looked at his sister. 'All right, Mandy. Out with it.'

'Out with what?' she deadpanned.

'Amanda Kennedy, I've known you for thirty-five years.'

'At least one year of which you wouldn't remember, because you were a baby at the time,' she retorted.

'Agreed,' he said, 'but I can always read your expression. So don't ever take up playing poker, will you?'

She sighed. 'I guess.'

Nick had known that tonight wasn't just about his sister giving him an update on his nephew's cancer treatment. Despite going through a messy divorce, Mandy still believed in love and happy endings. And all too often she tried to fix him up with someone she thought would be his perfect date. Nick had stopped believing in love years ago, and he'd learned the hard way that you couldn't be successful both in love and in your career. So after the break-up of his marriage he'd gone for the safe option and concentrated on his career.

No doubt this was another of Mandy's friends who really needed a plus-one for a dinner party and he'd fit the bill perfectly. OK. He'd help out, but he'd make it clear that he wasn't looking for a relationship. Nowadays he didn't do anything deeper than casual dating.

Then his sister said something he really hadn't expected. 'The Friends of the Hospital are doing a calendar to raise funds for the ward.'

He didn't need to ask which ward. The cancer ward. The one that had treated his nephew Xander for osteosarcoma. Well, he could do something to help there, too. 'If they're looking for a sponsor to cover production costs, count me in.'

Mandy reached across the table and squeezed his hand. 'Aww, Nick. I knew you'd offer to help before I could ask you. But they already have a sponsor for printing costs.'

'OK. What else do they need to cover? Distribution? Warehouse? Paying the photographer?'

'Um—not that, either. The photographer's doing it for nothing.'

'Then what?'

She took a deep breath. 'They want you to be one of the models.'

'Me?' He looked at her, totally shocked. He knew his sister had been under a lot of stress recently, but had she gone temporarily insane? 'Why?'

Mandy raised her eyebrows. 'Need I remind you that you actually got approached by a model agency when you were seventeen?'

'And I didn't take up their offer.' He might have considered it, to fund his way through university; but a couple of weeks later their parents had split up and life had disintegrated into chaos. Nick had forgotten all about the modelling offer and retreated into his studies. Concentrating on his books was what had got him through all the upheaval of his parents' divorce. Just as concentrating on his job had got him through the misery of his own divorce.

'Seriously, Nick—will you do it? They're looking for people who are connected with the ward.'

As Xander's uncle, he definitely had that connection.

'And they want people with interesting jobs.'

'A barrister isn't that exciting,' he said.

'Yes, it is. You look like a film star in your wig and gown.'

He rolled his eyes. 'Mandy, I'm just an ordinary guy.'

'Like hell you are. Apart from the fact that you're my little brother, which would make you special in any case, can I remind you that you're one of the youngest ever barristers appointed to being a QC?'

He grimaced. 'Why would anyone be interested in that?' About the only people who would even know what a QC was were people who had needed to brief one. Or maybe fans of certain types of TV crime drama.

'And you'd be helping raise money for the ward. Money they really need for new equipment.'

That was an unbeatable argument, and they both knew it. How could he possibly say no? This was to help other kids who were in Xander's position. And a little voice in his head added selfishly that maybe if he did it, then that would persuade Fate to give Xander a break and keep him in remission. And for that Nick would do almost anything.

'Will you do it?' she asked.

He closed his eyes briefly. 'All right.'

She smiled. 'Good. Thank you. I'll give your phone number and email to them, then—I'll do that now, if you don't mind, because they're waiting on my answer.'

'OK.' But Mandy was still hiding something, he was sure. 'And the rest of it?' he asked.

She blinked. 'What do you mean?'

'You're holding something back.'

She shrugged and tapped a message into her phone.

'Just save us both the time and tell me the rest of it, Mandy,' he said, leaning back and eyeing her over his glass of water.

'OK.' She sat back in her own chair and looked at him straight. 'Since you ask, you're going to be naked.'

'What?' He'd just taken a sip of water and he nearly choked on it. Naked? He must've misheard. No way would his sister have done this to him.

'You won't be *showing* anything,' she said.

'Define naked,' he said grimly.

'In court. Wearing your wig and robe.'

He shook his head. 'I'm afraid I can't do that, Mandy. The Head of Chambers would never agree to it.'

'Um, he already has.'

He blinked hard. Was he hearing things? Leo had already said yes? But—how? 'You what?'

'I talked to your clerk this morning,' she said. 'And he thinks it's a great idea.'

Now Nick was beginning to understand all the knowing smiles that had greeted him all afternoon. The news must've gone round chambers in ten seconds flat—gossip that juicy would never be ignored. And they'd all known that he didn't have a clue what was going on, making it even more fun for them.

'So what exactly did Gary say?' he asked, keeping his voice low and even and meanwhile planning how he was going to make his clerk grovel hugely in the morning.

'He put me through to your Head of Chambers. Then I told Leo all about it and he said he thought it was really a good idea, too. And he's getting clearance for us so you can do the shoot in the local court. He says he'll cover any photographic permission costs at the court himself.'

'Oh, good God.' With his boss on side, there was no way Nick could get out of it. He covered his face with his hands. 'Please tell me this is some weird, surreal dream. Please tell me it's a nightmare and I'm going to wake up. Preferably right now.'

'Nick, I've already told them you said yes,' Mandy said plaintively.

'That was before I knew I was going to be naked. This is a seriously bad idea, Mandy,' he said softly. 'I'm a senior barrister. I have to respect the dignity of the court. Which doesn't mean posing naked—or near-naked—for a calendar shoot, no matter how noble the cause is.'

'But Leo said it would be OK. And… Nick, we need you,' Mandy pleaded. 'And it's not as if you're the only one with a responsible job. One of the surgeons at the hospital is doing it.'

'Which is publicity for his own place of work.'

'And I think there's an actor and a musician on their list. And a chef.'

'All of whom would get a career boost from the publicity,' he pointed out.

'Please, Nick. For me. And for Xander.'

'It doesn't look as if I've got much choice,' he said grimly. 'But promise me you'll never, ever pitch a stunt like this again.'

'I promise. I'm sorry, Nick.' She bit her lip. 'But the ward needs the money.'

Lack of money meant lack of equipment. Which in turn meant that some kids wouldn't get the treatment they so badly needed. And that meant that those kids might even die.

Which was Nick's worst nightmare regarding his nephew.

And he was in a position to change that. To give more kids a chance of life—the same amazing chance that Xander had been given. All he had to do was pose for one little picture that would help to publicise the cause and encourage people to donate.

One little *naked* picture.

It really went against the grain. But far worse was the thought of his nephew dying and the way it would shatter all their lives and devastate his elder sister.

'All right,' he said, blowing out a breath. 'But I need to double-check this with Leo myself, first, and make sure that he's absolutely clear on all the details. And if he changes his mind and says that I can't do it, then I'll sell calendars by hand for you—and I'm very persuasive, so I'll sell tons of them to everyone in the whole of Inner Temple and Middle Temple. Plus I'll also give a personal donation to match those sales. Double.' Time *and* money. They'd be a good alternative to posing naked for a calendar, wouldn't they?

And hopefully he'd be able to persuade his Head of Chambers that having one of his barristers naked and in the focus of the press might not be such a good idea…

CHAPTER TWO

AND OF COURSE Leo still said yes. Even when Nick pointed out exactly what was involved.

So, two weeks later, Nick found himself heading to the local Crown court. Leo had arranged for Court Number Two to be used outside the normal court working hours, though there was still a chance that Nick might bump into someone he knew who'd want to know what he was doing hanging round the court building when he wasn't in a trial—especially when he looked as scruffy as he did right now.

S. J. Thompson, the photographer, had sent him a couple of very business-like texts to arrange the photo shoot and explain that Nick needed to dress casually and remove anything that might cause a mark on his skin—socks, collars, waistbands and the like—at least two hours before the shoot.

For putting him through something as embarrassing as this—not to mention the teasing he knew he'd get from his colleagues when the calendar actually came out—Fate had *better* keep Xander safe, Nick thought grimly.

When he got to the court, carrying his court attire in its usual boxes, there was nobody waiting outside. The only person he could see in the lobby was a woman who looked to be in her late twenties or so, wearing black trousers, a black silky short-sleeved top and black shoes. Her blonde hair was cropped so short as to be almost a military cut. She didn't look remotely like the man Nick was here to meet.

She looked up from her book, then closed it, stood up and walked towards him. 'Nick Kennedy, I presume?'

He blinked. Was she the photographer's assistant or something? 'Yes.'

'Thank you for being on time. I'm S. J. Thompson—though you can call me Sammy, if you like.' She held out her hand for him to shake.

'*You're* S. J. Thompson?' Even as the words came out, he realised how dim they sounded. And how stupid of him to assume that the use of initials meant that the photographer was male.

She gave him a slight smile. 'I'm afraid so.'

Clearly he wasn't the first to have made that mistake. 'I—er—nice to meet you,' he said, feeling totally wrong-footed.

And, when he shook her hand, awareness zinged through every pore. Sammy Thompson was the most striking woman he'd met in a long time. And that severe haircut only served to highlight how pretty and feminine her face was. There was nothing masculine at all about her. Her mouth was a perfect rosebud, and he found himself wanting to trace her lower lip with his fingertip. Worse still, he could picture himself doing that before leaning in and kissing her. Lightly at first, a touch as light as a butterfly's wing, and then deepening the kiss as she responded…

He shook himself mentally. Oh, for pity's sake. This was *business*. OK, maybe not the normal kind of business he'd conduct here in the court, but it was still business. And he wasn't exactly known for having ridiculous flights of fancy.

But he did feel uncomfortable right now.

It was nothing to do with sexism—as far as he was concerned, it was how you did your job that mattered, not what your gender or your sexual orientation or your religion was—but Sammy's gender made this situation a little more difficult. Because it meant that now he was going to be stripping off in front of a woman he'd never met before.

Either his doubts showed on his face or she was used to this reaction from the people she photographed, because she said softly, 'It's not going to be as bad as you think. And, if it helps, remember that I'll be seeing you simply as a life model rather than as an actual person. I don't tend to hit on my models.'

'I—yes. Of course. Sorry.' How long had it been since he'd felt in a whirl, like this? He was never this pathetic and woolly. And he really hoped he didn't look as if he was staring at her. He forced himself to look away. 'I believe we have Court Number Two booked.'

'My equipment's already in there, though I haven't set it up fully yet,' she said. 'Once we've decided precisely where you're going to stand, it won't take me long. Oh, and we really ought to cover the legal details now.'

Legal details? That got his attention.

'Firstly, I have public liability insurance, which covers any damage to person or property while we're in the location—not that there will be any—and secondly I'll need you to sign a model release form,' she said.

'It's pretty standard wording, but I'd still prefer you to read it thoroughly before you sign it.' There was just the slightest twinkle in her sea-green eyes as she added, 'Though I guess in your case I don't really need to tell you to ask me to explain any legal wording you don't understand.'

'Quite,' he agreed, trying to sound cool and professional. Even though Sammy Thompson was making him feel decidedly hot under the collar. What was it about her that made him feel like this?

'Shall we?' She gestured for them both to go in to the court room, and put a note on the door saying *Filming in progress: do not enter.*

'I take it you've worked in here before, or at least somewhere like this?' she asked.

'Yes.'

'Good. Then you'll be comfortable with the setting,' she said approvingly.

True, but he really wasn't comfortable with what he was about to do. 'Usually I'm fully dressed when I'm in this room,' he said.

She indicated his cases and suit carrier. 'This lot contains what you wear in court, I assume?'

He nodded. 'I brought all of it because I wasn't sure what you'd need.' Though he knew it would be a lot less than he would prefer.

'OK. Talk me through it,' she invited.

He took his work clothing out of the cases he'd brought with him, piece by piece, and laid each one in turn on the judge's bench. 'Tunic shirt, waistcoat, pinstripe trousers and frock coat.'

'You don't wear a normal business suit under your lawyer's gown?' she asked, sounding surprised.

'I did before I took silk,' he said. 'That is, before I became a QC—a Queen's Counsel.'

'Which is a senior barrister, right?'

'Yes. So that's why I wear the frock coat.' He took out the gown. 'And this.'

'And that gown's silk, I assume?' she asked.

'Yes.'

'May I touch it?'

He frowned. 'Why?'

'So I can move it about and see how the light affects it,' she said. 'Obviously I'll be careful with it. One of my best friends is a wedding dress designer, and I've taken most of the shots for her portfolio and website, so I understand how to handle material without marking it.'

'Ah. Of course.'

His fingers brushed against hers as she took the gown from him, and it felt as if pure electricity were running through his veins. What on earth was the matter with him? He never reacted like this. Especially to a complete stranger.

Maybe he was overreacting because he hadn't dated in a while, and his body's natural urges were making themselves felt because Sammy was really attractive. Well, tough. This was business and he really didn't have time for this. Behave, he told his libido mentally. You know relationships are a disaster zone.

She peered at the material carefully from several angles, then nodded in seeming satisfaction. 'OK. Do you wear lace at your collar, or am I thinking of something else?'

'That'd be ceremonial legal dress,' he said. 'Normally in Crown court a male barrister wears a wing collar that attaches to the shirt, and court bands.' He took them out of their cases for her.

'So the bands are the things that hang down like a two-pronged white tie?'

Despite himself, he smiled. 'Yes. Actually, they're symbolic. The Lord Chief Justice said back in the sixteenth century that they were two tongues. One for the rich, for a fee, to reward our long studies; and one without reward to defend the poor and oppressed.'

'I like that,' she said. 'So you defend the poor and oppressed?'

'I'm usually a prosecutor,' he said, 'but English barristers can defend as well as prosecute. I guess in either case I'd be defending my client's interests, and it's not for me to call them poor or oppressed.'

Sammy liked that little bit of humility. Given that Nicholas Kennedy QC was a top barrister, she'd half expected him to be a bit on the arrogant side, but she instinctively liked the man she'd just met. He had kind eyes, a deep rich brown. And, even though he clearly wasn't very comfortable with the idea of being part of a shoot for the charity calendar—especially now he knew the photographer was female—he'd obviously made a promise to someone and had the integrity to keep that promise.

She could see exactly why the committee had asked him to pose for their calendar. Talk about photogenic. His bone structure was gorgeous. He could've been a model for a top perfume house, advertising aftershave. It was rare to have that kind of beauty teamed with an equally spectacular intellect. And it made him almost totally irresistible.

But she was going to have to resist the pull of attraction. She was here to work, not to drool over the eye candy. Right now she was supposed to be putting the man at his ease. And hadn't she just told him that she never hit on her models?

Well, this wasn't going to be a first for her.

Be professional, she reminded herself. She wasn't going to let herself remember the little shiver of desire that had rippled down her spine when he'd shaken her hand. Or wonder how that beautiful mouth would feel against her skin. She was going to focus on her job.

Besides, he was probably committed elsewhere. He wasn't wearing a wedding ring, but that didn't prove anything. A man that beautiful would've been snapped up years ago.

'Your hair's very short,' she commented. 'Do you have a military background, or is the haircut necessary because you have to wear a wig in court?'

'It makes the wig a little more comfortable, yes,' he said. 'Speaking of which…' He took out the wig next.

There were short, neat rows of curls all the

way round the pale grey wig, and two tiny tails hanging down at the back with neat curls at the ends.

'The wig is what everyone associates with lawyers in court,' she said. 'You'll definitely be wearing that, and probably the gown—though I might do some shots without the gown as well.'

'What else do I get to wear?' he asked hopefully.

'Not the trousers, the coat or the shirt, I'm afraid. Even though they're nicely cut and made from good material.'

He flinched.

'You can wear the collar and tie thingies.'

She could see in his expression that he was dying to correct her terminology—but he didn't. Clearly he was resisting the temptation to be nit-picky and was trying to be co-operative. Teasing probably wasn't the kindest or most appropriate thing she could do right now.

'Thank you. I think,' he said.

She smiled. 'As I said, to me you'll be simply a life model.'

But she needed him to relax so the strain wouldn't show on his face when she photographed him. Given what he did for a living—and that he'd agreed to wear some of his court dress for the shoot—she guessed he'd be more comfortable talking about his work. 'Talk me through the court layout, so I can decide where to put you.' Even though she knew perfectly well where she was going to ask him to stand. She'd done her research properly, the way she always did before she took a portrait.

'Right in front of us is the judge's bench.'

'Where he bangs his gavel, right?'

He laughed. 'I think you've been watching too many TV dramas. English judges don't use gavels.'

She knew that, but he didn't need to know that she knew. It looked as if her plan to make him more comfortable was working. Except, when he laughed like that, it made him look sexy as hell—and that made it much more difficult for her to keep her part of the bargain, to be detached and think of him as a life model.

Not that Sammy was looking for a relationship right now. She was too busy with her job, and she was fed up to the back teeth with dating Mr Wrong—men who ran for the hills in panic, the second they learned about her past, or who saw themselves as her knight in shining armour and wrapped her so tightly in cotton wool that she couldn't breathe. None of them had seen her as a woman.

Then again, she wasn't really a whole woman any more, was she? So she couldn't put the blame completely on them.

And after Bryn had finally been the one to break her heart, Sammy had decided that it would be much easier to focus on her family, her friends and her job and forget completely about romance.

Though the wedding she'd photographed a couple of months ago had made her feel wistful; now both her best friends were loved-up and settled. And although she was really happy for both of them, it had left her feeling just the tiniest bit lonely. And the tiniest bit sorry for herself. Even if she ever did manage to meet her Mr Right, there was no guarantee of a happy ending. Not if he wanted children of his own, without any kind of complications. She couldn't offer that.

She pushed the thought away. Enough of the pity party. She had a great life. A family who loved her—even if they were a tad on the overprotective side—friends who'd celebrate the good times with her and be there for her in the bad times, and a job that really fulfilled her. Asking for more was just greedy.

'No gavel, then. So what else am I looking at?'

'OK. In front of the judge you have the clerk of the court, the usher, and the person who makes the sound recording of the trial or a stenographer who types it up as the trial goes along. They face the same way as the judge.' He walked over to the benches facing the judge's bench. 'This is where the barristers sit, though we stand when we're addressing the court. The defence barrister is nearest to the jury—' he indicated the seats at the side of the room '—and the prosecution barrister is nearest to the witness box. The solicitors sit behind the barristers, and at the back is the dock where the defendant sits. Over there behind the witness box you have the public gallery and the press bench.'

'So it'd make the most sense to photograph you where you'd normally stand in court,' she said. Exactly where she'd always planned for him to pose—and where her equipment just so happened to be waiting. 'OK. Can you stand there for me?'

'Dressed like this?' he asked.

She smiled. 'For the moment, yes—though

if you wouldn't mind putting on your gown, that'd help with the light meter readings.'

He shrugged on his gown and went to stand at the barristers' bench. She noticed that he was looking nervous again.

'You're really not going to end up on the front page of the newspapers with headlines screaming about "top barrister flashes his bits",' she reassured him. 'The point of the calendar is to sell gorgeous men posed artistically.' And Nick definitely fitted the bill on both counts. 'If the bench doesn't cover your modesty, so to speak, then you can hold a bunch of papers in a strategic place. Don't you normally have a bunch of papers with you in court, tied with a pink ribbon?'

'A brief,' he said. 'It's the instructions from my client. The defence has a pink silk ribbon and the prosecution uses white.'

Though he still didn't look convinced about the shoot.

She sighed. 'Look, just stand there for a second.'

As he did so, she took her camera body out of its carrying case, fitted a lens so she could take a quick photograph, then came over to show him the digital picture on the screen. 'This obviously isn't a proper composition—

for the real one I'll be quite a bit more nit-picky about the lighting and the lens—but it should be enough to prove to you that your dignity will remain intact. OK now?'

'Sorry.' He blew out a breath. 'I know I'm being ridiculous about this. I guess this just isn't the normal sort of thing I'd do in a day's work.'

'That's pretty much what everyone's said so far.' She grinned. 'Well, except for the actor. He didn't mind stripping off, but I guess he'd done it a few times before. All in the name of art, of course.'

'Of course,' Nick echoed, still looking uncomfortable.

'And what you do in court—you have a persona, and that's a bit like acting, isn't it?'

'A bit, I suppose,' Nick said. 'But, as I said, at work I'm normally wearing quite formal dress—not standing in the middle of the room, almost naked.'

'For what it's worth,' Sammy said, 'I think what you're doing is really special. It takes guts—everyone's happy enough to put their hand in their pocket and donate money to a good cause, but you're doing something out of the ordinary. Something that's going to make a lot more of a difference. And I bet whoever you're doing this for is hugely proud of you.'

'My sister,' he said, 'and my nephew.'

'The ward treated your nephew?' she asked softly.

He nodded. 'Xander's in remission at the moment.'

She guessed the bargain he'd made in his head: if he did this to help raise money, then Fate might smile on his nephew and keep him in remission. She knew her own sister had made the same bargain, and it was why Jenny had her hair cropped at the same time as Sammy did, every two years.

She wondered briefly why Xander's father hadn't offered to do the calendar shoot. Or maybe it was just that Nick had a more photogenic job. It was none of her business, anyway. She was just here to do the shoot.

'OK. I'm happy with that position. Now, there aren't any windows in here; plus we've got a notice on the door, so nobody's going to walk in on us. It's quite safe. So, while I'm setting up properly here, do you want to lose the clothes?'

No, Nick didn't want to lose the clothes. At all.

But he'd promised he'd do it, and he wasn't

going to break his word. 'What do you want me to wear out of the court dress?' he asked, drawing on his usual court demeanour and trying to sound as if he was completely unflustered.

'Wig, collar and bands, and we'll try some shots with the gown and some without,' she said. 'I take it you followed my instructions to avoid marks on your skin?'

'Yes.'

'Good. Let's do this.'

Nick felt incredibly self-conscious stripping off. Putting on the collar and bands without his tunic shirt felt *weird*. Though the silk gown was soft against his skin, and he gathered it in front of him to cover himself and went to stand by the bench.

'We'll do some shots sitting down, first,' Sammy said. 'I guess you need some papers spread out on the bench in front of you.'

Luckily he'd thought to bring a brief with him. He fetched it and sat down.

'Do you wear glasses?' she asked.

'No.'

'Pity. I should've thought to bring some frames with me.'

He frowned. 'Why do you want me to wear glasses?'

'To make you look clever.'

He wasn't sure if she was teasing him or not. Then he looked her straight in the eye and saw the mischievous twinkle. 'Very funny.'

'Yes, m'lud—or should I say Your Honour?'

He rolled his eyes. 'That's what I'd say to the judge. You'd refer to me as My Learned Friend.'

Her mouth quirked, and heat flooded his body. That impish smile transformed Sammy Thompson to a pure beauty.

And this was totally inappropriate.

He damped his feelings down. For all he knew, she was married or involved with someone. OK, so she wasn't wearing a ring, but that didn't mean anything. And he wasn't looking for a relationship anyway; the disintegration of his marriage to Naomi three years ago had put him off the idea of opening his life to someone else ever again. The one woman he'd thought was different. The one he'd thought had supported his ambitions and understood him. Yet it had all been a sham. That wasn't a mistake he intended to repeat. Even if he did find Sammy Thompson attractive, he wasn't going to act on that attraction. Dating seriously wasn't something he did any more.

He focused on posing for Sammy and following her instructions. He stood up, changing position when she told him to.

'OK. Now you can lose the gown for the next set of shots.'

'Are you quite sure about this?' he asked, wishing he were a hundred miles away.

'Tell you what, shy boy,' she drawled. 'Do the rest of the shoot for me without making any more fuss, and I'll buy you dinner.'

He blinked. Was she asking him out? 'Dinner? Why?'

'Because I've already shot two other models for the calendar today and I didn't have time for lunch, which means that right now I'm starving—I'll apologise now in case my stomach starts rumbling during the shoot. So I think we should have dinner while we look through the shots and you tell me which ones you approve to put forward to the Friends of the Hospital,' she said. 'Unless you have a girlfriend or a wife who'd have a problem with that, in which case please call her now and ask her to join us, because I really don't want to have to wait for too long before dinner.'

He shrugged slightly. 'No wife. No girlfriend.' And this was feeling more and more like agreeing to a date. Something that pushed him even further outside his comfort zone. He paused. 'Would it be a problem for your partner if you ate with me?'

'Not if I had one, because this is my job.'

So she was single. Available…

He squashed those thoughts. No, no and no. He didn't date any more. Not seriously.

'The quicker we get this done, the quicker I get food,' she continued, 'and the less likely it is that I'll get grumpy with you. You need to focus, m'learned friend. Lose the gown. And think yourself lucky.'

'Lucky?' He very nearly had to shake his head to clear it. Was she talking about *him* getting lucky?

'You're Mr December. I could've made you wear a Santa hat. Or pose holding a bunch of mistletoe. Or—' She flapped a dismissive hand. 'Insert a cheesy Christmassy pose of choice.'

Ah. *That* kind of lucky. Nothing to do with sex, then.

And would his head please, please start playing by the rules and stop thinking about lust and other inappropriate things? Because right now he was naked, and it would be impossible to hide his physical reaction to her.

'Noted,' he said dryly. He took off his gown, folded it neatly, and set it on the bench where it would be out of sight of her camera.

Wearing just his barrister's wig, collar and bands, Nick Kennedy was spectacular, Sammy thought. Broad shoulders, beautiful biceps, enough hair on his chest to be sexy without him looking like a total gorilla, and a definite six pack.

Mr December was going to be the best page on the calendar. He could probably sell the calendar all by himself.

But now he'd said there was no wife or girlfriend, she couldn't help wondering: how come a gorgeous man with a good brain and kind eyes was single? Was it because he was a workaholic and his girlfriends tended to get fed up waiting for him to notice them? Or had she missed some major personality flaw?

'What?' he asked, clearly noting that she was staring at him.

'Nothing,' she said, embarrassed to discover that her voice was slightly croaky. She really had to get a grip. The last thing she needed was for her skittish model to work out that she was attracted to him. And Nicholas Kennedy was bright. He couldn't be more than five or six years older than Sammy's own thirty years, and he was at the top of his profession. Scratch bright: that kind of background meant he had to be super-bright. So he'd be able to work it out quickly.

She got him to do a few more poses. To her relief, he'd relaxed enough with her by now to trust her, even when she moved round and took some shots from the side and some others from the back. And, oh, his back was beautiful. She'd love to do some proper nude studies of him. In a wood, looking for all the world like a statue of a Greek god.

Not that he'd agree to it. Not in a million years.

But a girl could dream…

'OK. That's a wrap. You can get dressed now,' she said, 'and by the time I've loaded everything on to my laptop we'll be ready to go to dinner.'

'The stuff I was wearing is hardly dressy enough for going out,' he said.

She laughed. 'As I wasn't planning to take you to the Dorchester or Claridge's, I think you'll be just fine.'

She put the memory card in the slot on

her laptop and downloaded the photographs while she packed away the rest of her equipment. Once she'd finished downloading the pictures, she saved the files. 'Is it OK for me to turn round now?' she asked with her back still towards Nick.

'Sure.'

Rather than putting on the ratty T-shirt and tracksuit bottoms again, he was wearing the white tunic shirt—without the collar—the waistcoat and his court trousers.

Sammy's heart skipped a beat. Right now, with his formal dress very slightly dishevelled, he looked as sexy as hell. She could imagine him with the shirt undone, especially as she'd actually seen his bare chest. If his hair was ever so slightly longer and someone had ruffled her hand through it to suggest that he'd just been thoroughly kissed, he'd look spectacular. In fact he'd go straight to number one in the Sexiest Man in the World list. She itched to get her camera out again. And this time she'd make him pose very differently.

'OK?' he asked.

No. Not OK at all. She was all quivery and girly, and that really wasn't good.

So she'd have to fall back on acerbic humour to hide how she really felt. 'Sure. Lucky,

lucky me—I get to have dinner with a half-dressed man.' Her mouth quirked. 'Are you really so vain that you couldn't go out to eat in an old tracksuit and T-shirt?'

'I'm not vain,' he protested. 'I just feel a little more comfortable in this than I do in the scruffy stuff.'

'It'd serve you right if I took you to a fast-food burger restaurant now—and then you'd really look out of place,' she teased.

'I'll bluff it. There's nothing wrong with burgers.'

Did he really expect her to believe that? She'd just bet he was the kind of guy who went for fine wines and Michelin-starred dining. 'When was the last time you went to a fast-food place?' she challenged.

'Last weekend, with my nephews,' was the prompt reply. 'Next question?'

Ouch. She'd forgotten about his nephews. If they were teens, like her own nephews, then she knew he'd be very familiar with fast-food places. She screwed up her face. 'OK, now it's my turn to apologise. Blame my rudeness on low blood sugar. Because I am a grumpy, starving photographer right now.'

He smiled, and she wished she'd kept her mouth shut. Stuffy and uncomfortable, she could deal with, but relaxed and sexy was another kettle of fish entirely.

Right now, Nick Kennedy could be very dangerous to her peace of mind.

'Let's go and eat,' Nick said, 'and you can show me how much of an idiot I've made of myself.'

He hadn't made an idiot of himself at all. He was utterly gorgeous and he'd be the star of the calendar—even more so than the actor and the musician who'd posed for her earlier in the week, because they were aware of how pretty they were and Nick wasn't. But Sammy knew she needed to keep her libido under control. She'd learned her lesson well, after Bryn.

No.

More.

Relationships.

Make that underlined and with three exclamation marks. And covered in acid yellow highlighter to make sure she didn't forget it.

'My car's outside,' she said.

'So is mine.'

She took a coin from her purse. 'Let's toss for it. The winner gets to drive. Heads or tails?'

'Heads.'

It was heads.

'My car, then,' he said.

'Do you mind if I bring my equipment with me?' she asked. 'I'd prefer not to leave it unattended, even if it's locked out of sight in my car.'

'It would make more sense,' Nick said, 'if we got a takeaway and ate it at my place. Then neither of us would have to worry about leaving expensive work equipment unattended in the car.'

'Why your place and not mine?'

He coughed. 'Because I just won the coin toss.' He paused. 'You can ring my sister and ask her to vouch for me, if you're worried about going to a stranger's flat.'

'A stranger who's willing to put himself out of his comfort zone to help raise money for an oncology ward, and whose day job means he skewers the baddies in court and gets them sentenced for their crimes? I think I'll be safe enough with you,' Sammy said. Plus all her instincts were telling her that Nick was one of the good guys, and her instincts—except when it came to dating—were pretty good. 'But I'll follow you in my car. That makes more sense than getting the Tube back here afterwards.'

'You won't have to get the Tube back here. I'll give you a lift.'

'So you're going to drive home, then back here, then home again? That doesn't make sense either.' She took her phone out of her bag. 'Give me your address, just in case I get stuck in traffic and can't follow you over a junction or something, and end up having to use my satnav.' She tapped in the details as he dictated them. 'Great. Let's go.'

'Can I carry anything for you?' he asked.

She indicated his armful of boxes and carriers. 'I think you've got enough of your own, and anyway I'm used to lugging this lot about.'

'Fair enough.'

She took the notice off the court door, told the security team that it was fine to lock up, and packed all her equipment into her car. And all the time she was berating herself mentally. She must be crazy. Why hadn't she just done what she'd agreed with her other models and emailed him a choice of half a dozen photographs that she could go on to present to the calendar committee? Why was she letting him review the whole shoot with her?

The truth was because she wanted to spend

more time with him. Because she was attracted to him.

But she also knew that her relationships were a disaster area. She had a three-date rule, because agreeing to more than that risked her having to tell the truth about her past—and in her experience men reacted badly to the information. Besides, she was pretty sure that Nick Kennedy was a total workaholic who wouldn't have time for a girlfriend—that was still the only reason she could think of why someone as gorgeous and good-hearted as him would be single—so it was better not to start anything. So she'd be sensible and professional when they looked at the photographs. They'd grab some food; and then she'd say a polite goodbye and never see him again.

Pity.

But, since Bryn, Sammy had learned to be sensible. It was the safest way.

And she was never getting her heart broken again.

CHAPTER THREE

AS HE DROVE back to his flat, Nick wondered if he'd just gone completely crazy. Why on earth had he invited Sammy Thompson back to his flat?

Then again, she'd had a fair point about not leaving expensive equipment unattended in a car. Horsehair wigs and silk barrister gowns weren't exactly cheap, either, and he wouldn't want to leave them in his car—just as she clearly hadn't wanted to leave her camera equipment in hers.

Out of the few dates he'd been on since the end of his marriage, he hadn't invited a single one of his girlfriends back to his flat. And he was far too sensible to invite a complete stranger back to his flat.

Yet that was exactly what he'd just done. Today was the first time he'd met Sammy. He knew practically nothing about her, other than that she was a photographer and she'd been commissioned to shoot the calendar by the Friends of the London Victoria.

Then again, he had good instincts—except perhaps where his ex-wife was concerned, he admitted wryly—and he'd liked Sammy immediately. She was business-like and capable, and she had a sense of humour that appealed to him.

And he was going to have to ignore the fact that she was utterly gorgeous. Slender yet with curves in all the right places, maybe six inches shorter than his own six foot one, and she was strong enough to carry heavy boxes of photographic equipment around without it seeming to bother her. Her bright blonde hair—which he was pretty sure was natural rather than dyed—was cut in a short pixie crop that framed her heart-shaped face, and her sea-green eyes were serious when she was working and teasing when something amused her.

Then there was her mouth. A perfect cupid's bow. A mouth that he'd wanted to trace with the tip of his finger before exploring it with his own mouth…

This was bad. He hadn't waxed poetic over anyone like this for years—maybe not since he was a teenager. So he'd better get it into his head that Sammy Thompson was simply the photographer who was working on the charity calendar, and he'd probably never see her again after today. Except maybe if the ward held some kind of launch event when the calendar went on sale and they both happened to attend it, and then they could just be polite to each other.

Be professional, he told himself. Treat her as if she's a client, or a colleague. Keep it business-like, choose the photographs, and then you can just let her walk out of your life and go back to what you normally do. Work, being there for Mandy and the boys, and more work. A perfectly balanced life.

Sammy was glad that she'd taken Nick's address and put the postcode into her satellite navigation system before they left the court's car park, because as she'd half expected she ended up losing him at a junction. Following the satnav's directions, she ended up driving through one of the prettiest tree-lined streets in Bloomsbury, where the five-storey town houses all had wrought iron railings, tall white-framed sash windows that would let huge amounts of light flood into the rooms, and window boxes full of bright, well-manicured geraniums. She could see Nick's car towards the end of the street, and thankfully there was a parking space on the road behind it. Nick himself was waiting for her by his car.

When she climbed out of her car, Nick handed her a parking permit to place inside her windscreen. 'I'm sorry I lost you at that junction,' he said. 'I did slow down, but I couldn't see you behind me.'

'No worries,' Sammy said with a smile. 'That's precisely why I took your address.'

'Come in,' he said.

'And you don't mind if I bring all my stuff in?'

'That's fine.' He was still laden with his own cases, but even so he picked up the heaviest of her boxes and took it to the door of the Georgian house on the corner.

It was exactly the kind of building that made Sammy itch to get her camera out. The front door was painted black, with white columns and narrow bands of stucco either side to turn the entrance from a rectangle to a perfect square. Above the entrance was a filigree fanlight, the pattern within the arched window reminding her of a spider's web. The door knocker, handle and letterbox were all shiny brass, the front doorstep was scrubbed clean, and on either side of the step there was a bay tree in a black wooden planter, its stem perfectly straight and its leaves clipped into a neat ball.

Everything was discreet, tidy—and clearly wealthy without being ostentatious about it. It was a house that had been looked after properly.

Clearly her interest showed on her face, because Nick smiled. 'You like the architecture?'

'It's gorgeous,' she said. 'I have to admit, architectural detail is one of my biggest weaknesses. Especially windows like that one.' She indicated the fanlight above the front door.

'Come on up and I'll give you the guided tour.' And then he looked slightly shocked, as if he hadn't meant to say that.

Tough. He'd said it now, and Sammy wasn't going to pass up the chance to look round such a gorgeous building.

'My flat's the ground floor and first storey,' he said.

'Not the whole house?'

He smiled. 'I live on my own, so I don't really need a whole town house. The flat gives me enough room for work, guests and entertaining.'

Though even a flat in a building like this—and in an area like this—would cost an eye-watering amount, Sammy thought. Especially a duplex flat. It would be way out of her own price range.

'Let's base ourselves in the kitchen,' Nick said. 'We can order some food, and then I'll show you round.'

'Sounds good to me.'

Nick's kitchen was small, but perfectly equipped. It had clearly been fitted out by a designer and it was the kind of shabby chic that didn't come cheap, with distressed cream-painted doors and drawer fronts, light wood worktops and pale terracotta splash-backs and floor tiles. There was a terracotta pot of herbs on one of the windowsills, and an expensive Italian coffee-maker and matching kettle, both in cream enamel; apart from that, everything was tucked neatly away.

Either Nicholas Kennedy was a total neat freak, or he didn't actually use this room much himself, she thought.

She set her boxes on the floor next to the light wood table at one end of the kitchen and put her laptop on the table itself. 'Is it OK to leave these here?'

'Sure.' Nick opened a drawer and brought out a file. Sammy had to bite her lip to stop herself grinning when she realised that his takeaway menus were all filed neatly in punched plastic pockets. She'd bet they were in alphabetical order, too.

Clearly he didn't have a clutter drawer with menus and all sorts of bits and pieces stuffed into it, unlike everyone else she knew. He was a neat freak, then. But that didn't mean he was totally buttoned-up. After all, he'd agreed to do a naked photo shoot. Someone totally stuffy would've refused to do that.

'Would you prefer Indian, Chinese, or Thai?' he asked.

'I eat practically anything,' Sammy said, 'except prawns. Fish, yes; crustaceans, no. Other than that, anything you like, as long as it's here as soon as possible.'

'Because you're starving. Noted.' He gave her a slight smile. 'How about a mix of Chinese dishes to share, then? And I promise, no prawns.'

'That'd be lovely.'

'Crispy duck?'

'Love it. Thank you.'

She set up her laptop while he was ordering their meal.

'They'll be here in forty minutes,' he said. 'OK. I promised you a guided tour.'

Sammy didn't quite dare ask if she could bring her camera. 'Lay on, Macduff,' she said with a smile.

'Living room,' he said, showing her through the first door.

Like the hallway, it had a stripped pale wooden floor. There were two huge sash windows dressed with floor-length dark green curtains; the walls were painted dark red and there was an antique-looking glass chandelier hanging from the high ceiling. It looked more like the effort of a designer than personal choice, Sammy thought.

The sofas were all low, upholstered in dark green leather and looked comfortable, and there was a light-coloured wooden coffee table in the middle of the room, set on a green silk patterned rug. There was a black marble fireplace with a huge mirror above it, reflecting the chandelier and the state-of-the-art television and audio-visual centre. Between the two sash windows, there was an enormous clock with a white face and dark roman numerals. There were plenty of silver-framed photographs on the mantelpiece, which she assumed were of his family.

But what really grabbed her attention was the painting on the wall. It wasn't exactly out of place, but she would've expected the designer to choose a couple of period portraits or maybe some kind of still life, to go with the rest of the decor. This painting was a modern landscape of a bay at dusk where the sea, cliffs and sky blurred together in the mist. It was all tones of blue and grey and silver—really striking. 'That's beautiful,' she said.

'Yes. I liked it the moment I set eyes on it,' he said.

So this was his taste rather than his designer's? She liked it. A lot.

Just as she had a rather nasty feeling that she could like Nick Kennedy rather a lot, if she got the chance. He was more than easy on the eye, and she liked what she'd learned about him in the short time she'd known him.

He ushered her in to the next room. 'My office.'

It was another room with dark red walls and stripped wood floors, but this time the curtains framing the two huge sash windows were cream voile and the patterned silk rug in the centre was dark red. The chandelier was wrought iron, and one wall was completely filled with books, most of which she guessed would be legal tomes. There was a desk against the opposite wall, teamed with what she recognised as a very expensive office chair—the kind she'd dreamed about owning but couldn't justify the price tag—and a state-of-the-art computer sat on his desk.

She could imagine him working here, with a bunch of papers spread out on the desk, his elbow resting on the table and his hand thrust through his hair while he made notes with a fountain pen. Because Nicholas Kennedy was definitely the kind of man who would use a posh pen rather than a disposable ballpoint.

'Dining room,' Nick said, showing her the next room.

Like the other rooms, the dining room had stripped floors; but it was much lighter because the walls were painted cream rather than dark red. There was a huge mirror above the white marble fireplace, reflecting the light from the sash windows and the antique glass chandelier. A light-coloured wooden table that seated eight sat in the centre of the room, teamed with matching chairs upholstered in cream-and-beige striped silk, which in turn matched the floor-length curtains. The silk rug here was in tones of cream and beige. She loved the room; she could just imagine sitting on the window-seat with a book, sunning herself while she read.

And there was another striking piece of art on the wall—a close-up of a peacock with its tail spread, and it looked as if it was painted in acrylics. 'The colours are glorious,' she said softly, enjoying the splash of orange among the turquoise, blues and greens. And it was so very different from the other picture; clearly Nick's taste was diverse.

But the artwork that really made her gasp was in his bedroom. The room was large, but for a change not painted dark red; it had blue and cream Regency striped wallpaper, floor-length navy curtains, stripped floors and a dark blue silk patterned rug to reflect the curtains.

She couldn't take her eyes off the black and white photograph that had been sliced vertically into three and framed in narrow black wood: a shot of the steel and glass roof of the Great Court at the British Museum. 'That's one of my favourite places in London.' And she had quite a few shots of that roof in her own collection. 'I adore that roof.'

'Me, too,' he said. 'It's the pattern and the light.'

'Did you know that no two panes of glass in the roof are the same?' she asked.

'No, but now you've said it, I'm going to have to look.'

'There are more than three thousand of them,' she pointed out. 'And the differences are tiny. It's only because of the undulations.' But the sudden light in his eyes now they were talking about art made her wonder. 'Did you ever think about being an artist or an architect rather than a barrister?'

He smiled. 'Absolutely not. I can barely draw a straight line with a pencil.' And then he changed the subject, making her wonder even more. 'Given that I already know you're starving, can I make you a coffee and offer you some chocolate biscuits to tide you over until the takeaway arrives?'

'That would be lovely. Thank you,' she said. 'Your flat's beautiful. Though I wouldn't have put you down as someone who'd choose dark red walls.'

'An interior designer organised most of the place for me just before I moved in,' he admitted. 'Maybe my living room and office are a little dark.'

Just a tad, but she wasn't going to be rude about it. '"Strikingly masculine" is probably the official phrase,' she said with a smile.

He ushered her back to the kitchen. She sat at the table and opened the file of photographs on her laptop while he made the coffee; and then he brought over two mugs of coffee and a plate of really good chocolate biscuits.

'Help yourself,' he said. 'And don't be polite. You said you'd missed lunch.'

'Thank you,' she said gratefully, and devoured two. 'These are scrumptious.'

'They're my sister's favourites,' he said. 'I keep a stock in for her.'

Nick was the kind of man who paid attention to details and quietly acted on them, she thought. She'd just bet he had a stock of his nephews' favourite treats, too. And the coffee was better than that served in most upmarket cafés; though, given that posh coffee machine sitting on his kitchen worktop, it wasn't so surprising. If you had an expensive machine, it stood to reason that you'd use good coffee in it. 'Would you like to see the photographs now?' she asked.

'Sure.' He viewed them in silence, then nodded with what she was pretty sure was relief. 'You were very discreet. Thank you.'

'The point is to raise money, not to embarrass people,' she said softly. 'And it's meant to be fun, so I think we should discount this one, this one and this one—' she pointed to them on the screen '—as you look very slightly uptight in them.'

'Agreed,' he said. 'I have to admit, picking out your own photographs is a bit…' He grimaced.

'It makes everyone squirm. It's much, much easier to look at someone else's photographs and choose the best ones in a set than it is to choose your own,' she said.

'Which ones would you choose?' he asked.

'Honestly? This, this and this.' She pointed them out. 'Mainly because of the expression on your face. You look more relaxed here.' And really, really sexy, which was the whole point of the calendar. Selling pictures of hot men to make money for the ward. Not that she was going to say it; she knew it would make him uncomfortable.

'OK. I'm happy with those ones,' he said.

'Great.' She took the model release form from her bag. 'So we'll put the shot numbers in here.' She wrote them down. 'Would you like to check that you agree with the numbers before you sign?'

He smiled. 'You sound like a lawyer.'

'I sound like a professional photographer who likes to get things right,' she corrected.

He checked the numbers on the form against the numbers on her laptop, then signed the form. 'I'm impressed with what you did. Can I see any of the other calendar shots?'

Sammy shook her head. 'Sorry. Only the Chair of the Friends and the committee members she chooses to work with her on the project can see them until the proofs are printed,' she said.

'Fair enough. I was just curious.'

'About the other models?' she asked.

'About your work,' he said, 'given the way you reacted to that picture of the British Museum's roof.'

'Ah. If you want to see my portfolio, that's a different matter entirely.' She pulled up a different file for him. 'Knock yourself out.'

He looked through them. 'You've got a real mixture here—lots of people and a few landscapes.'

'They tend to go with profiles of people in magazines and Sunday supplements,' she said. 'That's my bread-and-butter work. So if the profile is of someone who's set up an

English vineyard, I'd take a portrait of that person and then whatever else is needed to illustrate the interview or article. Say, the vineyard itself, or a close-up of a bunch of grapes, or the area where the wine's produced or bottled.'

'What about the photographs you take for you?'

'What makes you think I don't take these ones for me?' she parried.

'Apart from the fact that you admitted that they were work, it was the look on your face when you saw the house—as if you were dying to grab your camera and focus in on little details. Particularly the fanlight window.'

'Busted,' she said with a rueful smile. 'Architecture's my big love—I never wanted to be an architect and create the buildings myself, but what I like is to make people focus in on a feature and see the building in a different light instead of just taking it for granted or ignoring it entirely.' And, although she'd never normally show her private shots to someone she barely knew, something about the way Nick looked at her made her want to open up. She went into another file. 'Like these ones.'

'They're stunning,' Nick said as he scrolled through them. 'And I mean it—I'm not just being polite. I'd be more than happy to have any of these blown up, framed and hung on my walls.'

She could see in his face that he meant it. And it made her feel warm inside. Some of her exes had scoffed at her private photography, calling her nerdy and not understanding at all what she loved about the architecture. And others had wanted her to give it all up so they could look after her—because a cancer survivor shouldn't be pushing herself to take photographs from difficult positions. Hanging off a balcony to get a better angle for her shot really wasn't the sort of thing a delicate little flower should do.

She'd wanted a relationship, not a straight-jacket. And being protected in such a smothering way had made her feel stifled and miserable, even more than when the men she'd dated had backed off at the very first mention of the word 'cancer'.

'So when do you take this kind of shot?' Nick asked.

'When I get a day off, I walk round London and find interesting things. And sometimes I go to the coast—I love seascapes. Especially if a lighthouse or a pier's involved.'

'And you put your pictures on the internet?'

'I have a blog for my favourite shots,' she admitted.

'So did you always know you wanted to be a photographer?' he asked.

'Like most kids, I didn't have a clue what I wanted to do when I grew up,' Sammy said. 'Then, one summer, my uncle—who was a press photographer before he retired—taught me how to use a proper SLR camera.' Nick didn't need to know that it was because she'd been cooped up in one place, the summer when she'd had treatment for osteosarcoma; she'd been bored and miserable, unable to go out with her friends because she had been forced to wait for the surgical wounds to heal and to do her physiotherapy. Uncle Julian had shown her how she could get a different perspective on her surroundings and encouraged her to experiment with shots from her chair. 'I loved every second of it. And I ended up doing my degree in photography and following in his footsteps.'

'A press photographer? So you started out working for a magazine?'

'For the first couple of years after I graduated, I did; and then the publication I worked for was restructured and quite a few of the staff were made redundant, including me.

That's when I decided to take the leap and go freelance,' she explained. 'Though that also means I don't tend to turn work down. You never know when you're going to have a dry spell, and I like to have at least three months' money sitting in the bank so I can always pay my rent.'

'And you do weddings as well?' He pointed to one of the other photographs.

'Only for people close to me. That one's Ashleigh, one of my best friends, on Capri last year.'

'It's a beautiful setting.'

'Really romantic,' she agreed. 'The bridesmaid is my other best friend, Claire. She and I went to the Blue Grotto, the next day. It was for a commission, I admit, but I would've gone anyway because the place is so gorgeous. You had to lie down in the boat to get through the entrance, but it was worth the effort. The light was really something else.' She flicked into another file and showed him some of the photographs. 'Look.'

'I like that—it's another of the sort of scenes I'd like to have on my wall,' he said.

She nodded. 'Like that misty seascape in your living room. That's the kind of thing I like to shoot at dawn or dusk. If you do it with a long exposure, the waves swirl about and look like mist.'

'That's clever,' he said.

She smiled. 'No. That's technique. Anyone can do it when they know how.'

When their food arrived, Sammy put her laptop away while Nick brought out plates and cutlery.

'Would you like a glass of wine?' he asked.

She shook her head. 'Thanks for the offer, but I'm driving so I'd rather not. A glass of water's fine, thanks.'

He poured them both a glass of water from a jug in the fridge—filtered water, she thought. Nick Kennedy clearly dotted all his I's and crossed every T.

'Help yourself,' he said, gesturing to the various dishes in the centre of the table.

'Thank you.' She noticed that he eyed her plate when she'd finished heaping it. 'What?'

'It's refreshing, eating with someone who actually enjoys food.'

'That sounds as if you've been eating dinner with the wrong kind of person,' she said dryly. 'Most people I know enjoy food.'

'Hmm.'

She finished stuffing one of the pancakes with shredded duck and cucumber, added some hoi sin sauce and took a taste. 'And this is seriously good. I haven't had crispy duck this excellent before. Nice choice, Mr Kennedy.' She paused. 'As we're going halves on this, how much do I owe you?'

'My house, my hospitality, my bill,' he said. 'No arguments.'

'Thank you.' Though there was more than one way to win an argument. Maybe she could print one of her seascapes for him, the one he'd really liked, to say thank you for the meal. 'So you like modern art rather than, say, reproductions?' she asked.

'Some. I'm not so keen on abstract art, which probably makes me a bit of a philistine,' he admitted.

'No, you like what you like, and that doesn't make you a philistine—it makes you honest,' she said. 'And your taste is quite diverse. I'm assuming they're original artworks, given that one of them is acrylics?'

He nodded. 'I like to support local artists where I can. There's a gallery not far from my chambers. The gallery owner gives me a call if something comes in that she thinks I'll like.'

'That's fabulous. It means both the artist and the art-lover win. Well, obviously, and the gallery owner, because she gets her commission.'

'Something like that.' He paused. 'Can I ask you something personal?'

Her heart skipped a beat. From his body language and the way he'd relaxed with her, she had a feeling that the attraction was mutual. Was he going to ask her out?

And, if he did, would she have the courage to act on that attraction and say yes?

'Sure,' she said, affecting coolness.

'Your hair,' he said. 'What you said about me being in the military—is that why your hair's so short, too? You spent time in the Forces?'

The question was so unexpected that she answered it honestly before she realised what she was saying. 'No. I have a crop like this every two years.'

He blinked. 'Why two years?'

She could try and flannel him and say that it was a fashion statement, but he was observant. She was pretty sure he would've picked up the cues. 'Because it takes that long for my hair to grow twelve inches.'

He looked puzzled. 'Why do you need to grow your hair twelve inches?'

'Because seven to twelve inches is what they need for wigs,' she said softly.

The penny dropped immediately. 'You donate your hair?'

She nodded. 'There's a charity that makes wigs for kids who've lost their hair after chemotherapy. My sister Jenny and I have our hair cut together every two years. We normally get people to sponsor us as well, and the money goes to the ward so they can buy things for the kids. You know, things to keep them occupied and cheer them up, because being stuck in hospital isn't much fun—especially when you're a kid.' The hair cut before last had been on the actual day of Sammy's test results. She and Jenny had celebrated the news with a hair cut and a bottle of champagne.

'That's a really nice thing to do. I take it your sister's your connection to the ward?'

'Uh-huh,' Sammy said. It wasn't a total fib. Her sister was one of the connections. Just Sammy herself happened to be the main one. Not that Nick needed to know that.

'So that's why you're taking the photographs.'

She nodded. 'I take photographs for the ward every Christmas—so the families do at least get to have some Christmas pics together with their children, and with Santa for the younger ones. That's why Ayesha knew I was up to the job and would waive my fee, because I always do where the ward's concerned.'

'I assumed you were a photographic student who wanted to do it for his portfolio, and you'd been interviewed with half a dozen others.'

'No,' she said. 'Though you have a point about the portfolio. Maybe I should've given someone else the chance to work with me.'

'But then your styles would've been different,' he said.

'I guess. But I ought to think about that in future.'

When they'd finished their meal, Sammy refused the offer of more coffee. 'I'd better let you get on.'

Which Nick guessed was a polite way of saying that she needed to get on. And now, he thought, this was where she left and they'd say a polite goodbye, and they'd never see each other again.

Except his head and his mouth were clearly

working to different scripts, because he found himself asking, 'When's your next day off?'

'I'm actually on holiday at the moment,' she said. 'I'm doing the last four shoots for the calendar tomorrow and the day after, but other than that my time's my own.'

'You're using your holiday to shoot the calendar?' And yet she'd said she was a freelance who never turned work down. Her time off must be precious.

She shrugged. 'It's not a big deal.'

But she wouldn't meet his eye. And she'd said that her sister was her connection to the ward. So maybe she'd made the same kind of silent bargain with Fate that he had, Nick thought—do the job and it'd keep her loved one safely in remission.

'So, thanks for dinner. And for being patient at the shoot,' she said. 'I know it can be a bit wearing, being told exactly how to stand and moving your head or your shoulders just a fraction.'

'You were very professional and made it easy,' he said, meaning it.

This was his cue to say goodbye. But his mouth had gone into reckless mode. 'Would you spend the day with me on Sunday?' he asked. 'Maybe we could have lunch, and you could show me some of the places you really like in London.'

'Urban hiking, one of my American friends calls it.' She smiled. 'I'd like that. OK. But there's a string attached.'

He frowned. 'What?'

'You bought dinner tonight, so I'm buying lunch on Sunday. No arguments.'

He wasn't surprised; Sammy had already struck him as someone who was seriously independent. He wasn't going to argue for now, but he'd find a way to get round her reservations on Sunday. 'OK. What time?'

'Half past nine?' she suggested.

'OK. It's a date.'

Even though he'd promised himself he wouldn't date again. Because Sammy Thompson intrigued him. And he wasn't quite ready to say goodbye to her yet.

CHAPTER FOUR

'SO HOW WAS the photo shoot?' Mandy asked.

She sounded ever so slightly guilty, Nick thought. 'It was fine,' he reassured his sister. 'The photographer was nice. She put me at my ease, and she let me choose the shots to give to the committee.'

'*She?* But I thought…' Her voice trailed off.

'So did I,' Nick said wryly.

'Oh, no. It must have been so embarrassing, taking all your clothes off in front of a woman you'd never met before.'

Nick laughed. 'She was at pains to tell me before the shoot that she saw me only as a life model, not as a person.'

'Right.' Mandy sounded intrigued. 'So was she young? Old?'

'It's immaterial, Mandy. Don't even think about trying to match-make.' And no way was he admitting to his elder sister that he was seeing the photographer for lunch on Sunday. It probably wouldn't come to anything, anyway. By then his common sense would be back in place. He and Sammy would have a nice walk through the city together, talk about art and architecture, have lunch, and then not see each other again.

Except Nick discovered the next morning that his common sense was very far from being back in place. When he walked into the narrow lanes off Fleet Street to his chambers, he found himself looking at the buildings with a photographer's eye.

Sammy would love this area, he thought.

And she'd really love the hidden gem in the middle.

He couldn't resist texting her.

I have a bright idea for Sunday.

Details? she texted back.

Just bring your camera. Which Tube line are you on?

There was a short pause before she replied: Northern.

Meet you at Embankment Tube station at 9.30? he suggested.

Her reply was a smiley face and a slightly sassy note.

Hope good coffee is involved.

He grinned and typed back: It will be.

On Sunday, Sammy felt ridiculously nervous. This was her first date in months—and it was with someone whose working life and whole lifestyle were so very different from her own.

She'd liked Nick Kennedy instinctively. She was attracted to him. And it was definitely mutual.

But how would he react if she told him she'd had osteosarcoma as a teen?

She didn't think he'd be one of the men who ran for the hills—his nephew had the same condition, so he'd understand instead of panicking at the c-word. But would he be overprotective, the way her family was, making a big deal out of every twinge she felt and worrying that it might be the first sign of something more sinister?

And, if he was close to his nephews, did that mean he liked kids? That maybe he'd want some of his own, some day? That could be a problem, because—thanks to the demands of her treatment—she might not be able to have kids in the future. There were possibilities, but no actual definites, because she'd had to have her eggs frozen before her first chemotherapy—and IVF didn't come with a cast-iron guarantee that it would work.

Part of her wanted to make up an excuse and call the whole thing off. Not because she was a coward, but because over the years her boyfriends' reactions to the complications had worn her down. It had left her feeling less of a woman and more of a freak.

Though part of her was intrigued by Nick. He was a man with a buttoned-down, highly respectable job, and yet he'd actually posed naked for a charity calendar. That took guts; and it also hinted at an unconventional streak.

So maybe this could even be the start of something good. She'd have to take that leap of faith and try to trust that it wouldn't go the same way as her last few relationships had.

Maybe Nick Kennedy was different.

But, until she knew him a little better and could work out what his reaction would be, she'd keep quiet about the fact that she'd had bone cancer and was in remission.

* * *

Nick's heart skipped a beat as he saw Sammy at the Tube station. Again, she was dressed completely in black, though this time her T-shirt was more of a vest top, in a nod to the warm September weather, and she wore a silver necklace decorated with deep green beads that matched the studs in her ears.

And she looked stunning.

Not that she seemed to realise she was turning heads. That was something else he liked about Sammy Thompson. She was just herself, comfortable in her own skin. And that in itself made her easy to be with.

He greeted her with a kiss to her cheek. 'So you're being the Mysterious Woman in Black again?' he teased.

She smiled at him. 'I never thought about it before but, yes, I probably do wear too much black. Sorry. I guess it's a hangover from art college.'

'Don't apologise. Actually, it suits you,' he said. 'And I like your jewellery.'

'The green stuff? It's malachite,' she said. 'One of my art school friends became a jeweller when she graduated. I love Amy's work—all the strong lines and the colours. She uses very different semi-precious stones, too.'

'My sister likes that kind of thing, and she's got a birthday coming up. Perhaps you can give me your friend's details and maybe she can design something for me,' he said.

'Sure I can. Remind me when we stop for coffee—and I haven't forgotten that you promised me good coffee.'

'I did indeed.' He smiled at her. 'Shall we?'

Together they walked out of the Tube station, then headed down the Embankment with the Thames on their right.

'So where are we going?' she asked as he turned left and took her into a maze of narrow passageways.

'This is Inner Temple—one of the Inns of Court,' he explained.

'Where you work?'

He was pleased that she'd realised that. 'Yes. We're not going to my actual office, but I thought you'd like to see some of the area around it.' He led her into a courtyard. All the way round, there were dark brick buildings with tall sash windows and stone doorways. At each end of the courtyard was a white stone arched entranceway, and in the middle were trees, slatted benches and stone troughs containing bright pink geraniums.

'This is absolutely gorgeous,' she said. 'Is

it OK to take photographs here, or do I have to ask permission from someone?'

'It's fine as long as they're not for commercial use—then you'd need to talk to the media relations team first,' he said.

'Do you mind…?'

'Be my guest,' he said with a smile. He watched her as she looked around the courtyard and bent down to take various shots, moving position to change the angle of whatever had caught her eye. It had never occurred to him to do that; whenever he'd taken a photograph, he'd just framed a snap in the viewfinder.

Which was probably why his photographs were snaps and hers were a true art form.

'This was a really good choice, Nick,' she said. 'I like this place. A lot.'

And he thought that she might like what he was about to show her even more. 'Come this way,' he said, and led her through the archway. In the next courtyard was a church built of honey-coloured stone; part of it was completely round, with a smaller round tower perched on top.

'This is the original Crusader church in London—one of the four remaining round churches in England,' he said softly. 'And the reason I brought you here now is so you can explore it as much as you like before the Sunday service starts.'

'I had no idea this was even here,' she said, looking entranced. 'So we can actually go inside?'

He nodded. 'And it's got the Templar effigy tombs. I think you'll like them.'

She did. Not just the round church itself, but also the way the blues, purples and reds from the sunlight coming through the stained glass windows shone onto the dark marble pillars surrounding the Templar effigy tombs. This was her idea of the perfect day—and it had come from a very unexpected source.

'That's William Marshal. He served under four English kings, and was the regent for Henry III,' Nick explained as they stood in front of the tombs. 'Next to him is his son William.'

Stone effigies that were nearly a thousand years old, darkened by age, portraying knights wearing their mail armour, holding a shield and sword, with dogs at their feet. Sammy was entranced by them, particularly the little dogs, and took plenty of detail shots.

'I love this church. It's so peaceful,' she

whispered. 'Though inside it doesn't look as old as it actually is.'

'It was badly damaged in the second world war during the Blitz,' Nick whispered back, 'so it had to be restored. But I can show you something really, really old.'

It turned out to be a Norman doorway with a rounded decorated arch, with beautiful geometric ironwork spreading across the wood. Again, Sammy took plenty of photographs, focusing on the details that caught her eye.

'Come with me,' Nick said, and took her into the gardens.

There was a long, tree-lined avenue that Sammy found irresistible, and she made him pose in the centre of it.

'This is the Broadwalk,' he said. 'The London plane trees were planted here in Victorian times.'

And in the Peony Garden there was an ancient wall and an iron railing with wisteria tumbling down it. 'It's amazing that these gardens are smack in the middle of the city and only a few steps away from the Thames,' Sammy said. 'They're stunning. I thought I knew London pretty well, but I had absolutely no idea they were here.'

'Most people don't—though the gardens

are open to the public,' Nick said, 'and it's the perfect place to chill out on a summer lunchtime. If I'm not in court, I'll sometimes eat a sandwich out here. It's a good place to think, too, when you're stuck on some knotty legal problem.'

Sammy found the brass sundial in the centre of one of the gardens equally fascinating. 'Why is there a Pegasus in the middle of the sundial?' she asked.

'It's the symbol of Inner Temple. It's said that it was chosen for Robert Dudley.'

'The guy Elizabeth the First was in love with?'

'At the time, he was her Master of the Horse,' Nick said. 'He took part in the Christmas revels here in the middle of the sixteenth century, and his followers all wore the symbol of Pegasus. It's thought to come from there.'

'It's a beautiful piece of brasswork,' she said. 'Though I still think Dudley was a bit of a baddie. It was a little bit too convenient how his wife fell down the stairs and broke her neck. So did Amy Robsart trip or was she pushed?'

'We'll never know the truth,' Nick said.

She paused. 'Would you have defended

Robert Dudley in a court of law if he'd been up on a charge of murdering his wife?'

He didn't hesitate. 'If I was asked to, yes.'

She looked at him. 'Would you defend someone you absolutely knew was a criminal?' Because that was something she really couldn't get her head round. 'How could you defend someone you knew was guilty?'

Nick smiled. 'That's the first question everyone asks a barrister. First of all, in law, everyone is presumed innocent unless proven guilty. Secondly, everyone has a right to representation and we're not allowed to refuse to represent someone just because we don't like them, or because we don't believe in their case,' he explained. 'Barristers work under strict rules of ethics, and we're subject to the law. So if my client's guilty, I can't say in court that he's innocent, and I can't call anyone to give false evidence on his behalf, because that's perjury—I'd be struck off.'

'So would he get away with it?'

'It's the prosecution's job to prove the case to a jury so they're absolutely sure that the person in the dock committed the crime. The jury has to hear from both sides for the justice system to work properly,' Nick said. 'So as a barrister I care about my client having the same human rights and entitlements as anyone else.'

OK, so Nick was professional. But what about the ethics he'd spoken of earlier? What about doing the right thing? 'But if they'd admitted to you that they'd done whatever they'd been accused of?'

'Then I would advise them to plead guilty to the charge, because the truth would come out in court,' he said simply.

'And if they said they were still going to plead not guilty?'

'Then I could walk away, because my first duty is to the court. And I could also refuse to take the case if I was going to be a witness in the case, because there would be a conflict of interests.' He shrugged. 'Though sometimes innocent people appear guilty, and sometimes guilty people appear innocent, so it's really important that both sides are heard properly and all the evidence is put to the jury so they can reach a verdict.'

'So you wouldn't try to get your client off if they were guilty?' That made her feel better about the situation.

'Guilt isn't actually that black and white,' he said.

She frowned. 'How do you mean?'

'OK. Supposing I have a client—let's call him Tom—who's been accused of taking an expensive pen from a shop.'

'That's theft,' Sammy said promptly.

'Only if he intended to deprive the shop-owner of the pen permanently and dishonestly. Supposing he'd taken it accidentally and was on his way to give it back? Or maybe someone had threatened him—if he didn't take the pen, then that person would hurt someone he loved, which means he took it under duress. Or maybe,' Nick continued, 'Tom's only nine years old—which means he's under the age of criminal responsibility. Or he has dementia, to the point where he's not responsible for his actions and didn't realise he'd taken the pen.'

Sammy looked thoughtfully at him. 'So if Tom did take the pen, in those cases he wouldn't actually be guilty of theft.'

'Exactly. Guilt's a really tricky question,' Nick said. 'As I said, it's important that all the facts are known so the jury reaches the right verdict. Both sides have to be heard for the system to work properly.'

'You really love your job, don't you?' she asked. She could see his passion for it in his expression and hear it in the way he talked about it.

'Guilty as charged,' he said with a smile. 'Though not everyone gets that.'

If you had workaholic tendencies, it could play havoc with your relationships if your partner didn't understand how important your job was to you. Sammy knew that from experience. Was that why Nick was single? Because his girlfriends got fed up with coming second to his job all the time? Not that it was any of her business. She wasn't going to be pushy and ask. 'I really love my job, too,' she said, smiling back. 'There's nothing wrong with that.'

'I'm glad you get it,' he said softly. 'And there's something else I wanted to show you.' He took her back through to the maze of buildings.

'Old-fashioned street lamps,' she said with delight when they came to a stop in front of one. 'They're gorgeous. I love that shape—like the lanterns you see on Christmas cards. I can imagine people bustling past wearing top hats and capes and crinoline dresses.'

'Absolutely right, because this is the Victorian bit. These are working gas lamps,' he said. 'It's really atmospheric at night—like being back in Dickens' time. In fact, there are several bits of Middle Temple that he described in his books.'

With the stucco-fronted buildings and the narrow passageways, she could imagine it. 'This is amazing. You work in such a beautiful area, Nick.'

'I'm very privileged,' he said. 'And I promised you good coffee. Do you think it's too early for brunch?'

Sammy glanced at her watch. 'Whoops. Sorry. I had no idea I'd spent so much time photographing things. I'm afraid I can get a bit carried away. I…' She blew out a breath. 'Sorry.'

'Hey, no need to apologise. It was my idea to bring you here, and I'm really glad you liked it as much as I hoped you would,' he said, his eyes crinkling at the corners.

'Coffee and brunch,' she said, 'is a great idea. And, remember, we had a deal. It's my bill. No arguments.'

He looked as if he wanted to protest but, to her relief, he nodded. 'OK. Let's go this way.'

Nick had had a feeling that Sammy was going to be stubborn about paying her share. So had her ex been the controlling type who never listened to her? He couldn't think of any reason why someone as vibrant and gorgeous as Sammy Thompson would still be single, other than that someone had let her down. Badly.

His own track record wasn't great. And he didn't believe in love. So it wasn't fair of him to let this continue, see where things took them—because the chances were that she'd end up hurt. They'd have lunch and then he'd find a nice way of saying goodbye. Because, after all, it wasn't her fault; *he* was the problem.

He walked alongside her, half lost in thought. His hand brushed against hers once, twice, making his skin tingle. The third time, he ended up catching her fingers loosely between his. She didn't pull away, but she didn't look at him or make a comment, either.

Shy?

Weirdly, he felt the same. Like a teenager holding hands with his girl for the first time. And it was a very, very long time since anyone had made him feel like that. Enough to make him rethink his earlier decision. Would it be so bad, seeing where things went? Would it necessarily mean that one or both of them would get hurt? Could he take the risk?

Eventually they reached the café he'd had in mind. 'Is this OK with you?' he asked.

She looked at the menu in the glass case by the door. 'Very OK, thank you. Though it's going to be quite hard to choose, because I like absolutely everything on the menu.'

Again, he found her attitude to food so refreshing; his last couple of dates had been with women who were so focused on watching what they ate that they forgot to enjoy it. Meaning that he hadn't enjoyed his food, either. And he'd made polite excuses not to see them again.

The waitress greeted them as they walked through the door, showed them to a quiet table for two, and took their order for coffee while she gave them time to browse through the menu.

In the end, Sammy sat back in her chair and sighed. 'I just can't decide between the hazelnut waffles with berries and Greek yoghurt, or the eggs Florentine—or the scrambled eggs with smoked salmon and sourdough bread,' she finished, looking rueful. 'And I don't quite have room for all of them.'

'There are two ways of sorting that out,' he said.

'Which are?'

'Either we come here for brunch again and the next time we choose whatever we don't have today,' he said. 'Or we order two different dishes and share them.'

Or, better still, do both. Because, the more he got to know Sammy, the more he liked her and the more he discovered that he wanted to spend time with her. Even though this wasn't the way he normally did things.

'If we share,' she said, 'what do you suggest?'

'The smoked salmon and the waffles.'

'Done,' she said. 'And freshly squeezed blood orange juice as well as the coffee.'

'Sounds perfect,' he said.

When the waitress came back, Sammy ordered for them. Nick wasn't quite used to that, but he rather liked her independent streak.

She sighed happily once she'd taken a sip of her juice. 'This is almost as good as Venice.'

'Venice?'

'When we had breakfast on the Grand Canal,' she said. 'It was amazing. We sat there watching the gondoliers at the stand next to us. One of them noticed and actually serenaded us—we loved it.'

'Who's "we"?' he asked.

'Me, Claire and Ashleigh. Claire and Ash knew each other from school, and I met Claire at art school—she was studying textiles and I was studying photography. We were the Terrible Trio.'

'Were?' he prompted.

'They're the ones in the wedding pictures I showed you. The bride and the bridesmaid in Capri—that was Ash getting married last year, and Claire got married in the spring this year.' She shrugged, and gave him a super-bright smile. 'Obviously I still get to spend time with them when I'm in London. But we won't be going on holiday together any more, just the three of us.'

Something she'd clearly miss. Meaning that Sammy was feeling just a little bit lonely right now? he wondered. He felt lonely, sometimes. When he woke at three in the morning, the bed feeling way too wide and nobody to cuddle up to. And then his father's words from all those years ago would echo in his head. *Love's not reliable, the way work is. Give your job your heart and you'll get to the top. Give love your heart and it'll just cheat on you and break you.*

With age and maturity, Nick had come to realise that his father had been speaking from hurt and anger at the disintegration of his marriage. And Edward Kennedy had never recovered from the divorce—he'd buried himself in work, and moved to Brussels to take his career ambitions further when Nick was halfway through his degree. Edward had done well for himself and reached the top of his particular tree, but Nick often thought his father was lonely and there was a gap in his life.

It wasn't the kind of life Nick wanted for himself—all work and no love. He'd wanted to have both. He'd met Naomi and she'd seemed to understand his drive to be the best at what he did. She'd encouraged him. He'd thought he had it all.

But then he'd come home early and found out that his marriage wasn't what he thought it was. His father's words had turned out to be all too true: because she'd cheated on him and broken his heart. Just like the way his mother had done to his father. Or maybe some of that had been his own fault, for paying too much attention to his work and not enough to his wife—even though at the time he'd thought she was OK with the hours he worked.

He pushed the thought away. Not here. Not now.

When their food arrived, Nick noticed that Sammy went straight for the waffles.

'Aren't you supposed to eat the savoury stuff first and then the sweet?' he asked.

She shook her head. 'Haven't you heard? Life's short, so eat dessert first. It's a good philosophy.'

He thought of Xander and guessed that she was thinking of her sister. Wanting to push away the sadness, he said, 'Can I be nosey and look at the photographs you took earlier?'

'Sure.' She took her camera out of her bag and handed it to him. Again, their fingers touched and adrenalin rippled through him. From the brief widening of her eyes, Nick thought it might just be the same for her, too. Instant attraction. Something he had a feeling neither of them really had time for. And yet something about Sammy made him want to explore this thing between them further. Even though he didn't do love any more. Or maybe it would be different with Sammy, because she loved her job as much as he loved his. And she was direct. He didn't think she'd say one thing and mean another, the way Naomi had.

'These photographs are amazing,' he said. 'I'd never really noticed the kind of details you picked out. The stonework, the windows, the ironwork. You've made me see my workplace in a completely different way.'

'It's what I do,' she said simply. 'The same as you made me think a bit differently this morning, when we talked about people being innocent or guilty.'

'It's what I do,' he said. 'Sammy, are you busy this afternoon?'

'I've got nothing planned. Why?'

He decided to take the risk. 'Because I've really enjoyed spending time with you and I'm not really ready for that to end just yet.'

'Oh.' There was the faintest slash of red in her cheeks. 'Me, too,' she said, her voice ever so slightly croaky.

'Given that we're just round the corner from Trafalgar Square, I'm tempted to suggest going to the art gallery,' he said. 'But it kind of feels wrong to take a photographer to an art gallery.'

She laughed. 'Don't worry about that. I never need an excuse to go to the National Portrait Gallery. That's not work. It's pure pleasure.'

'And you love your job anyway,' he finished.

'Like you. And I'm guessing you get nagged

by your family as much as I do about overdoing things,' she said.

'My sister's favourite words are, "You work too hard."' He rolled his eyes. 'But how else are you really going to be good at your job and get to the top of your profession unless you put the hours in?'

'Absolutely. I guess in some areas you could get to the top by nepotism, but it wouldn't mean that you were any good at your job,' she mused. 'And I want to be the best photographer I can be.'

Her views were so like his own. Nick had a feeling that he'd just met the one woman who might actually understand him. Then again, he'd made that mistake before. He'd thought that Naomi had encouraged his ambitions—to the point where he'd considered easing back on his hours to spend more time with her and start a family. And yet he'd ended up making the same error as his dad and his sister. He'd put his trust in someone who seemed to see things his way on the surface, but had a hidden agenda. Someone weak, who'd lied to get her own way.

'Nick?'

'Sorry. Wool-gathering.' He forced himself to smile. 'Let's go to the gallery.'

When she excused herself to go to the toilet, he asked the waitress for the bill. Except he discovered that Sammy had beaten him to it and already paid it on her way to the ladies'.

'Thank you for brunch,' he said when she came back to their table.

'Pleasure. But it was my turn anyway,' she said, 'because you bought the takeaway, the other night.'

He couldn't argue with that. But it was refreshing to be with someone who believed in fair shares instead of expecting to be treated all the time.

On the way to the National Portrait Gallery, they ended up holding hands again. This time, Sammy slanted Nick a sideways glance, at exactly the same time that he looked at her.

She burst out laughing. 'Is it just me, or do you feel seventeen again?'

'Something like that,' he said, and tightened his fingers round hers. 'I feel as if I should have greasy hair that's badly cut, acne, and be quoting terrible poetry at you.'

She laughed. 'I bet you were a beautiful teen.' And then she blushed. 'Um, that's with my photographer's head on.'

'I'll accept the compliment very happily,'

he said. 'For the record, I bet you were a beautiful teen, too.'

'Nah. I was very ordinary,' Sammy told him with a grin.

He didn't believe that at all.

They spent the afternoon wandering round the gallery, and Sammy taught him how to read a portrait. 'The whole point of a portrait is to tell you about the subject. With the older paintings, the background's important and you need to look at what the person chooses to be painted with. In modern photographic portraits, you try to stop the background noise coming through and concentrate on your subject.'

There was a mischievous glint in his eye. 'I love it when you talk technical.'

She grimaced. 'Sorry. I can be very boring on my pet subject.'

'I'm not bored in the slightest. This is totally new stuff to me.' He smiled at her. 'Besides, I rambled on enough about law earlier.'

When she'd said how she loved her job, too. She'd understood something about him that Naomi never had. And it was crazy that it made him feel so warm inside.

'Do you have any portraits on display here?' he asked.

She laughed. 'Sadly, I'm not *quite* in the same league as David Bailey or Lord Lichfield. Maybe one day.'

'What's your favourite portrait you've taken?' he asked.

She looked thoughtful. 'I can probably name you half a dozen. But my absolute favourite is probably Freddy, the free runner.'

'You mean, one of those people who run around London and jump off rooftops?' he asked.

'According to Freddy, it's all about expressing yourself without limiting your movement—but yes, that's what it looks like. To get the interview and the portrait, the journalist and I went with him on a free run. He said you know who you are when you know how your body moves and what you're capable of doing. That if you learn to overcome obstacles in your environment you'll also learn how to overcome obstacles and stress in your daily life—and that fascinated me.'

'So you actually did the jumping off roofs bit with him?' Now that he hadn't expected.

'Not with my camera, no—the insurance would never have covered that kind of risk.' She smiled. 'But I did have a go when the journo looked after my camera.'

He raised an eyebrow. 'So are you brave, or are you a thrill seeker?'

'Neither,' she said. 'Life's short, so it's always worth taking the chance to experience something new, even if it seems a bit scary at first. Because that way you push yourself beyond your boundaries and you live life to the full—you don't get left with a pile of regrets at the end.'

'That's a good philosophy,' he said. 'So what's on your bucket list?'

For a moment he thought he saw her flinch. But it must've been his imagination. Or maybe it was a phrase that made her think about her sister. 'Sorry. That could've been phrased better.'

'Things I really want to do before I die.' She pursed her lips. 'Top of my list would be the chance to go to the edge of the earth's atmosphere—the bit where you see the blue curved line of space and all the blackness above. I'd love the chance to see that for myself and photograph it.' She looked straight at him. 'How about you? What's on your list?'

'Most of the places I want to see are in the middle of political turmoil right now,' he said, 'so it's not sensible to travel there. But on the doable list, I'd love to see the whales and polar bears in Canada. And see the Northern Lights.'

'Book the trip,' she said immediately.

Yeah. Except he wanted to share it with someone. 'When work isn't quite so busy,' he said, knowing that it was a feeble excuse.

'Being busy at work is fine,' she said softly. 'But it's important to remember to take time to play as well. To give yourself a chance to refill the well.'

Clearly his expression said that he thought that was totally flaky, because she grinned. 'I just believe in living life to the full. Work hard and play hard.'

He persuaded her to let him buy her coffee and cake in the gallery's café. When they'd finished, he said, 'May I see you home?'

'Thank you, Nick, but I'm an adult. I'm perfectly capable of getting myself home.'

There was a slight edge to her voice that surprised him. He'd thought they'd had a good time together. Clearly it was time to back off. 'Sorry. I was brought up to be a bit old-fashioned.'

'Courtesy—yes, I can understand that. Sorry for biting your head off.' She took a deep breath. 'Let's just say in the past my family's tried to wrap me up in cotton wool, and that drives me crazy.' There was a flash of panic in her eyes, gone so fast that Nick thought he might've imagined it. And then Sammy added, 'I guess it comes from being the baby of the family.'

Nick was the baby of the family, and nobody had wrapped him in cotton wool. When his mother's affair had come to light, his sister Mandy had been away at university and Nick had been left alone with his father—who'd been too hurt and angry to put a filter over his words. Edward Kennedy had said an awful lot of bitter, unhappy things that the teenaged Nick could've done without hearing.

He shook himself. Now wasn't the time to dwell on that. 'A photographer who's actually tried free running and dreams of going to the edge of space is the last person who'd want to be wrapped in cotton wool,' he said.

She looked relieved that he actually understood her. And then she looked him in the eye. 'We could always go for the compromise.'

'What's that?'

'Walk me to the Tube station?' she suggested.

'Works for me,' he said.

And he was pleased that this time she was

the one to tangle her fingers with his as they walked.

At the entrance to the Tube station, he turned to her. 'I've had a really nice day. Thank you.' He bent his head, intending to kiss her politely on the cheek—but somehow his lips ended up brushing against hers. Once, twice. Clinging. Exploring the softness of her mouth, the sweetness.

And it made him feel as if an electric shock had run through him.

When he pulled back, he could see the shock and surprise in her own eyes, so clearly it had affected her in the same way.

'Nick. I…' The words dried up and she shook her head helplessly.

'Yeah. Me, too,' he said softly. And, because he could see just the faintest bit of panic on her face, he backed off. 'See you later.' Even though he had the strongest feeling that he might not. And he didn't look back once as he headed on the half-hour walk back to his flat.

Sammy really hadn't expected that kiss. She didn't think Nick had intended to kiss her like that, either. He'd probably been aiming for her cheek—just as she'd been doing. Except then they'd both turned the wrong way and their mouths had accidentally collided.

She brooded about it all the way home.

Part of her didn't want to risk another relationship where she'd get let down.

And yet she'd told him her view on life. *It's always worth taking the chance to experience something new, even if it seems a bit scary at first. Because that way you push yourself beyond your boundaries and you live life to the full—you don't get left with a pile of regrets at the end.*

Dating Nick Kennedy was a scary prospect. One she wasn't sure she was brave enough to handle. What if he was disgusted by her scars and it made him back away? He wouldn't be the first. And, even if he wasn't repulsed by her leg, would she be enough of a woman for him? It was a bone-deep fear that she hadn't even discussed with her sister and her best friends. She knew they'd tell her she was being ridiculous and they were probably right, but that didn't shift the fear. The fact that she'd have difficulty conceiving—that if she met someone who wanted to have a family with her, they'd have to go through IVF using her frozen eggs, and there was no guarantee it would work—made her feel less of a woman. In her head, she knew it was stupid, but in her heart she couldn't help worrying about it.

But, if she walked away from Nick, would she end up with a pile of regrets?

Was this sudden burst of loneliness just a reaction to the fact that Claire and Ashleigh had both got married and she was the only one of the Terrible Trio who was single now? Or was it something more?

There was only one way to find out.

She texted him.

Very carefully.

Thank you. I had a really good time today.

He took his time in replying.

Me, too.

Was he being polite? Or was he being wary, given that she'd bitten his head off so unfairly?

Bravery time again. And this would be their second official date, so it was safely within her three-dates-and-end-it rule. She could do this. Keep it casual. Unthreatening. She tapped into her phone.

Maybe we could do something next week, if you're free.

That was the crunch suggestion. If he made an excuse and backed off, so would she. If he didn't…then maybe they could have some fun together.

He took even longer replying, this time. And she only realised how tense she was when her phone beeped and she saw his message.

Day or evening?

Either. I'm still on holiday next week. Nothing planned.

His reply was swift.

Am in court for at least three days but can do evenings.

Good. How are you with heights?

Instead of texting her, this time he called her. 'What do you have in mind? Is this something to do with free running?'

'No. Just heights. Something off my bucket list that I hope you'll enjoy.'

'The top of the Shard?' he suggested. 'Sure. Heights aren't a problem.'

'Not the Shard. Something else,' she said. 'Dress casually. I'll text you with the times and directions when I've booked it. *Ciao.*'

And then she hung up before she made a fool of herself.

CHAPTER FIVE

ONCE SAMMY HAD booked tickets for the outing she'd planned, she sent Nick a cheeky text.

M'learned friend, do you possess such a thing as a pair of jeans?

Clearly he was in court, because he didn't reply until lunchtime. And then he called her rather than texted her. 'Of course I own a pair of jeans, Sammy. Why?'

'Because I need you to wear them when you meet me on Thursday night. Trainers would be good, too, but they're not essential.'

'Jeans and trainers? Why? What are we doing?'

'Something fun,' she said. 'Because as I told you before, I believe in working hard, but I also believe in playing just as hard.'

'Fair enough. Are you at least going to tell me the location, or am I supposed to be developing my mind-reading abilities?'

She laughed. 'North Greenwich Tube station. And that's all you need to know for now. I'll text you the time.'

'Hmm,' Nick said, but she could hear the smile in his voice.

When Nick met Sammy on Thursday evening, she did a pirouette in front of him. 'I hope you notice that I'm not wearing black today,' she said.

She was wearing faded jeans, which clung to her like a second skin, a hot pink T-shirt, and canvas shoes that matched her T-shirt. And Nick was slightly shocked to realise how much he wanted to carry her off to his flat and peel her clothes off her. Very, very slowly.

'You look very nice,' he said, hoping that his thoughts weren't showing on his face and that she hadn't developed mind-reading skills. 'So where are we going?'

'The O2 Arena. We're booked in for the sunset climb,' she told him. 'I've already bought the tickets and this is my idea, so don't even *think* about offending me by offering to pay. Got it?'

'Yes, ma'am,' he said, saluting and clicking his heels together.

'Good. I'm glad you know your place, m'learned friend.'

And he loved the teasing glint in her eyes. With Sammy, he was starting to rediscover his sense of fun—something he'd lost after the break-up of his marriage, except for the time he spent with his nephews. 'So we're actually walking over the top of the Dome?'

'Yep. You were the one talking about bucket lists. This happens to be on mine. One of my best friends is totally scared of heights, but you said you were OK with them, so I thought I'd dragoon you into doing it with me.' She paused and frowned. 'Oh, wait. You haven't done this already, have you?'

'No.' Though this was definitely something that his nephews would love to do, he thought. Maybe it was something he'd suggest doing with them. Maybe he'd ask Sammy to join them—though he didn't know whether she actually liked children. Plus it was way too soon to suggest meeting his family. This was, what, their second date? Yeah. Way too soon. They needed time to get to know each other, first.

Live for the moment, he reminded himself. 'I'm looking forward to this.'

'Me, too.' She looked gleeful. 'This is going to be huge fun.'

He agreed. Particularly because he was going to be sharing the experience with her.

After a safety briefing with the guides, they joined the rest of their group in putting on their climb suits and boots. Next they put on a harness with a latch that they'd been told to clip to the walkway; and finally they climbed the stairs up to the suspended walkway.

The person at the front of the line stumbled partway up the steep incline, and the walkway rippled with the impact. The person in front of Sammy stopped dead, clearly worried, and Sammy had to stop short.

Nick almost collided with her and rested his hands on her shoulders to steady them both. 'OK?' he asked Sammy.

'I'm fine,' she said. 'Apparently this happens a bit, especially on the way down. I'm sure we'll both be fine.'

The gradient levelled out, and finally they found themselves in the viewing platform on the centre above the Dome. Sammy took her mobile phone out of her pocket and took snaps of the panoramic view. Nick recognised the cable car, Canary Wharf, the Shard and the Gherkin, along with Royal Greenwich and the sculpture at the Olympic Park.

But best of all was the sunset, just to the side of the buildings of Canary Wharf. He could see exactly why this had been on her bucket list. It was a photographer's dream view.

'This is an amazing view,' he said.

She beamed. 'I hoped it would be like this—and I love the way all the skyscrapers are lit up, too, now it's dusk. Hey, can I take a selfie with you?'

He laughed. 'That sounds *really* weird coming from a professional photographer.'

'Don't knock it. A good selfie can still be a good shot. If you hold your arm out far enough and zoom in, then you're not going to end up with a bulbous nose or big ears.'

'Bulbous nose?'

She laughed. 'Like that shot where the monkey stole that camera from the photographer and managed to take a selfie. I've seen a few of those in my time.' She took a few snaps of them together on the edge of the walkway, with the iconic masts from the Dome sticking out on either side of them. And Nick enjoyed the fact that he got to put his arm round her, even if they were both in climb suits and he wasn't actually touching her skin.

'So now we're up here,' Sammy said to their guide, 'do we get to do the James Bond bit now, minus the bullets?'

'Sliding down the side of the Dome, you mean?' He laughed. 'I'm afraid that would be a no.'

'Pity,' she said, and clipped her harness back on the walkway to start the descent.

At the bottom, once they'd changed out of their climb suits and boots and walked away from the area, Nick teased, 'What with your yen for outer space, the free running stuff and now this, I think you were totally bluffing about bravery and you're really a thrill seeker at heart.'

'No. The free running stuff was work, anyway, and I haven't actually done it since. I just think it's a good idea to get out of your comfort zone every so often, because life is short and you need to appreciate every second of it,' she said. 'In fact, I have a very good idea right now…' She stood on tiptoe, cupped his face with her hands, and pressed her mouth to his.

Her lips were warm and soft and she tasted

of strawberries. And Nick couldn't help responding, wrapping his arms tightly round her and nibbling at her lower lip to persuade her to deepen the kiss.

Sammy Thompson made his head spin.

And he couldn't remember the last time he'd reacted so strongly to someone. He'd always thought of himself as careful—that he'd get to know someone over a few months before going to bed with them. But Sammy made him want to take all his brakes off and he wanted to make love with her right now. He wasn't sure if that was more exhilarating or frightening.

'Great idea,' he said when she finally broke the kiss. 'Apart from the fact that my head's totally scrambled now, thanks to you.'

'So you're outside your comfort zone?' she asked.

'Yes and no.' He stole another kiss. 'I think I could get to like this very much indeed. You?'

She fanned herself. 'I don't normally do this sort of thing with complete strangers.'

'We're not complete strangers now. Plus you've seen me naked,' he pointed out, 'which puts you at rather an unfair advantage.'

To his amusement, her face went bright

scarlet, clashing with her T-shirt. 'Nothing untoward was on show when you modelled for me,' she reminded him.

'I was naked, so it still counts. And I think this means I need to get to see you naked, to even things up.'

Her eyes were sparkling. 'Oh, do you now?'

He pulled her closer and nibbled her ear. 'That was the best idea I've had all day.' She was still deliciously pink. And he noticed that she wasn't making excuses and backing away. Anticipation skittered through him. Were they both about to break their own rules and fast-track to the next stage?

'I think we should feature you on the front cover of the calendar,' she said thoughtfully. 'Because, with your bare chest and your abs, we'll sell tons of copies for the ward.'

Which answered his question. This was teasing banter, not a statement of intent. Best to keep it playful, then. He groaned theatrically. 'OK. Shutting up now. Do you have to rush off, or shall we have dinner?'

'Dinner would be good,' she said. 'Shall we go to one of the restaurants here?'

'Here's fine. And dinner's on me, seeing as it was my idea and you bought the tickets to the climb.'

'Thank you,' she said with a smile.

They went to one of the bars inside the Dome, and looked through the menu.

'You're going to choose dessert first, aren't you?' he asked.

She wrinkled her nose. 'Yes, but it looks as if most of the puddings on the menu are chocolate.'

'Problem?' he asked.

She nodded. 'I hate chocolate puddings.'

'You don't like chocolate?' He was surprised. Every female he knew loved chocolate.

'No, I love chocolate,' she said, 'but I don't like chocolate puddings or chocolate ice cream. And I already know that makes me weird. I've been told that often enough.'

He grinned. 'Someone rather wise once told me that you like what you like and it doesn't mean you're a philistine—or, in this case, weird.'

She laughed back, clearly recognising that he was throwing her words back at her. 'I guess.'

She chose the salted caramel cheesecake—the only non-chocolate pudding on the menu—and they ordered a mix of sharing plates between them: ginger and lemon chicken, pulled pork, sweet potato fries, quinoa salad and stuffed peppers.

'What do you want to drink?' he asked.

'They can apparently mix a cocktail to suit you,' she said. 'And I'm really torn between a glass of Prosecco and a cocktail.'

'You could always have a cocktail based on Prosecco, and that way you get the best of both worlds,' he pointed out. 'Why not ask the barman? And I'll join you.'

Once they'd told the bartender what they'd chosen to eat, and Sammy explained that she wasn't much of a spirits drinker, he made them a cocktail of Prosecco mixed with ginger liqueur and limoncello.

'Excellent choice, m'learned friend,' she said to Nick with a grin after the first sip. 'I like this.'

'Me, too,' he agreed.

The food was just as good but the company was even better. Nick found himself relaxing with Sammy, laughing and talking about a complete mixture of subjects. Every so often, his fingers brushed against hers as they chose something else from their sharing platter, and adrenalin fizzed through his veins.

Plus there were those kisses. He couldn't get them out of his head. Her mouth was beautiful, her lips soft and warm, and he wanted to kiss Sammy again. Explore her. Find out where she liked being touched, where she liked being kissed. What made her curl her toes with pleasure.

There was definitely something special about Sammy Thompson. But would she be prepared to take a chance on him? Nick still hadn't worked out why she was single. She was bright, she was charming, and she made him see the world in a slightly different way. Someone, he guessed, must have hurt her and made her wary of relationships.

But maybe she could learn to trust him.

And maybe he could learn to trust her.

Because she wasn't like Naomi. Sammy struck him as very straightforward and honest. She wasn't the sort to spin a web of lies and turn someone into the bad guy when he hadn't actually done anything wrong.

After their meal, they walked hand in hand back to the Tube station. 'Sammy, I know you're old enough and tough enough to look after yourself, but this time will you please let me see you home to your front door?' he asked. At her raised eyebrows, he gave her a rueful smile. 'OK, I admit—it's because I've enjoyed tonight and I want to spend a few more minutes with you, and seeing you home feels like a good excuse.'

'And once you see me to my front door, then I'm supposed to invite you in for coffee?' she asked.

'It's not essential,' he said, 'though it would be nice.' He paused. 'And, if you offered, I'd accept.'

'Even though the coffee's not going to be made with a posh Italian coffee machine like yours?' she tested.

He laughed. 'You could give me a chipped mug of decaf instant coffee made with long-life milk that was almost out of date and that would be absolutely fine.'

She laughed back. 'No way—with a coffee machine like yours, you're used to the best and you might even verge on being a coffee snob. And none of my mugs are chipped, thank you very much.'

But she agreed to let him walk her back to her front door. It turned out that she lived in a small flat in Camden, among a row of terraced houses painted ice cream colours. Cute—and the area suited her, he thought. Vibrant, with something interesting round every corner.

'I'll give you the guided tour of the flat,'

she said. 'It's going to take us all of two minutes—and that's provided I talk a lot while I show you round.'

He smiled. 'Sounds good to me.'

She hadn't been exaggerating that much; her flat was compact and much, much smaller than his. All the floors were stripped and varnished wood, but that was the only thing their flats had in common. Her walls were all painted cream and the windows had neutral-coloured roman blinds rather than floor-length curtains. Though he guessed that made it easier to focus on the artwork; there were framed photographs grouped together on the walls that seemed to have either a similar theme or a similar colour.

'Are these all your own pictures?' he asked.

She nodded. 'I change them round every so often. But it's nice to use the shots rather than just leave them languishing out of sight on my hard drive.'

Her kitchen was open plan. 'I guess it's fairly self-explanatory—I use the dining table as a desk as well as to eat,' she said.

'It's a nice room,' he said. 'Comfortable.' The other half of the room was the living room and contained a sofa, a stereo system, a bookcase, a cupboard where he guessed she kept most of her photographic equipment, and a small television.

Her bathroom was only just big enough to contain a bath with a shower over it, the toilet and a sink; there wasn't a window, but the room was small enough for the overhead light to keep things bright. Her bedroom was equally bijou, with just enough room for a double bed with an iron frame, a small pine bedside cabinet, and a matching chest of drawers and wardrobe.

And he suddenly had the clearest picture of being in that double bed with her, curled up together and talking after they'd made love. Her face would be flushed with passion and her eyes sparkling. And he couldn't resist spinning her into his arms and kissing her until he felt dizzy.

'Well, now,' she said when he broke the kiss, sounding flustered.

'Sorry.'

She lifted an eyebrow. 'Are you?'

'For kissing you, no,' he admitted. 'For being pushy, yes.'

She smiled and stroked his face. 'I don't think either of us knows how to handle this. I don't usually invite men home after a second date. But here you are.'

'I don't usually invite complete strangers home, either,' he said. 'But I invited you back to my place after the shoot.'

She laughed. 'You don't strip off in front of strangers, either. But you did for me.'

It would be oh, so easy to pick her up and carry her to her bed. Suggest that he stripped for her again. Better still, suggest that she undressed him. Very slowly. With a lot of kissing in between.

But rushing things would just make life way too complicated.

He needed to cool things down. As in right now, before he did something reckless and they both got burned. 'Talk to me,' he said. 'Tell me about your job. Does it mean a lot of travelling?'

'I go wherever the photograph needs to be taken,' she said, ushering him back to her living room and then switching on the kettle to make coffee. 'Sometimes it's in London, but often it's further afield.' She lifted a shoulder. 'I've done some work in LA, some in New York, and some on various film locations. The best bit is when I get a chance to explore while I'm away and take some shots for myself, too.'

'Like your architectural stuff?'

She nodded. 'And seascapes.'

'So do you have a dark room and an office somewhere?' he asked.

She shook her head. 'Most of my work is digital, so I don't really need a dark room. But occasionally I borrow my uncle's, if I've been experimenting with arty shots and want to do it the old-fashioned way. There's something special about watching the shot develop on the paper.'

'And is it like they show you in the movies, with trays of liquids and a red light?'

'It's called a safe light, and it can be brown or red,' she said. 'Basically, ordinary light will ruin any unexposed film or photographic paper, whereas safe light means that you can see what you're doing but it won't wreck your work.'

'Sounds like a sensible solution,' he said.

'Though you don't have to have a special room to be a dark room,' she said. 'My bathroom doesn't have an outside window, so in theory it wouldn't take much to turn it into a dark room, provided I block out all the light round the door. And I could use my bath as a bench for the chemicals.'

He looked at her, surprised. 'But wouldn't they ruin your bath?'

'No, because you wash the chemicals away too quickly for them to do any damage—besides, the bath is the same kind of plastic as the trays.'

'So how does it work?'

'Basically you have four trays set up,' she explained. 'You expose the photographic negative onto the paper—the length of time you expose it controls what you see on the final image—and then you put the paper into developer trays so you can actually see the image. Once it looks exactly how you want it, you move the paper from the developer tray to the stop bath, so the picture doesn't develop any more. From there you move the paper to the fixer so you can look at the image in normal light later without it being ruined; and finally you rinse the paper in water to get rid of the last bits of chemicals.'

'And then you peg it up on a line to dry?' he asked.

'Just like in the movies. Yup.' She smiled. 'Actually, I love making black and white prints. I could take you to Uncle Julian's and show you how it's done sometime, if you like. It's magical when you see the image emerging, like a ghost at first and then getting stronger. And it's fun playing about with different contrasts, and different sorts of paper.'

'No. You have a passion for your job,' he said softly, 'and it shows.'

And he really wanted to see that passion in her eyes again.

Except he wanted to be the one to put it there. Like he had when he'd kissed her a few minutes ago.

When she finished making coffee, she came to join him on the sofa and set her mug on the floor. And that was the perfect cue for him to slide his arm round her shoulders. From there it was easy to twist round to face her, and to brush his lips against hers. Her mouth was soft and sweet and giving, and she slid her hands round his neck to draw him closer.

The next thing he knew, he was lying full length on her sofa, she was lying on top of him, and his hands were splayed against her back, underneath her T-shirt.

Her skin was so soft, so warm. Touching wasn't enough. He wanted to see, too.

Which was crazy. He never behaved like this, so out of control. He didn't do love. And he didn't want to hurt Sammy. He should back off. Now.

Except he couldn't.

He blew out a breath. 'Sorry. I'm taking this a bit too fast again.'

Her face was flushed and her eyes were sparkling. 'You and me both.'

'I'm sorry. I don't normally behave like this,' he said.

'Neither do I.' Her face was rueful. 'I might say outrageous things, but I don't tend to walk the talk,' she admitted.

'There's just something about you that makes me want more than I should ask for,' he said softly, holding her closer because he wasn't quite ready yet to relinquish the feel of her skin against his fingertips.

'Me, too. But, Nick, this probably isn't a good idea. Our lifestyles are too different.'

'Actually, they're probably too similar,' he corrected. 'We're both workaholics.'

'I guess so.'

He stole a kiss. 'So maybe it could work between us. But I agree. We need to cool this very slightly. Much as I'd really like to scoop you up and take you to your bed right this very minute—and believe me I've wanted to do that all evening—I can't do that, because I don't actually carry condoms around with me.'

'I don't have any either.'

His heart skipped a beat. Was she saying that, if she'd had condoms, she would've been fine with him taking her to her bed? For a second, he couldn't breathe.

'Rain check,' she whispered, and climbed off him.

The sensible thing, Nick thought, would be for them to sit at opposite ends of her sofa. Except her sofa was so compact that even when they tried it in tacit agreement, they were still close enough to touch.

Take it down a notch, he told himself, and took her hand instead.

'I'm trying to take it slower,' he said by way of explanation.

She smiled. 'OK. Let's pick a safe subject. We did something on my bucket list this evening. What's on yours, apart from polar bears, whale-watching, the Northern Lights and some places that are too dangerous for tourists?'

Making love with you.

Not that he was going to say that out loud.

And he was still a bit stunned that she'd actually remembered what he'd told her.

He thought about it for a while. 'A proper afternoon tea in a very posh hotel,' he said.

'With a cake stand and a silver teapot and someone playing the piano in the lobby.'

'Oh, come off it,' she scoffed. 'You're a barrister and you work in the middle of London. You must've done that before.'

'Actually, no. My clients don't generally tend to take me to tea at a posh hotel,' he said mildly, 'and in the afternoons if I'm not in court then I'm in my chambers, up to my eyes in paperwork. If I'm *very* lucky I might be able to sweet-talk my clerk Gary into making me a mug of tea—but usually we take turns, so whoever puts the kettle on in the kitchen usually checks to see who else wants a cuppa.'

'Seriously? You don't have a secretary?'

'Barristers have clerks,' he said. 'The clerks are responsible for the admin and business activities of the chambers. So Gary would do some secretarial things, like arranging meetings, invoicing solicitors for fees and planning case timetables in detail, but he also looks after three more barristers as well as me. He doesn't have time to wait on my every whim—and he wouldn't do that anyway,' he admitted with a grin. 'If I asked him to go and put the kettle on, he'd tell me I was old enough and ugly enough to make my own cuppa, he was already busy making phone calls on my behalf, and his is white with three sugars while I'm at it, thank you very much.'

'Right.' She smiled as if she was imagining the scene, then looked at him. 'I can't believe you've never had a proper posh afternoon tea.'

'I take it you have, then?' he asked.

'Oh, yes.' Her eyes lit up. 'Birthdays, red letter days, and any other time I can find an excuse to do it.'

'Seriously?'

'Provided the cake isn't chocolate. Then I have to talk people into swapping with me. But posh tea, dainty finger sandwiches, scones with jam and clotted cream, yummy little savouries… Yeah, I love all that. It's so decadent and such a treat. Like going out for breakfast. I think I'd rather do that than go out for dinner, even. It feels more special.'

He'd enjoyed sharing brunch with her. And he had a feeling that this particular item on his bucket list would be even more enjoyable if he shared it with her, especially as she sounded so enthusiastic about it. 'Right then, Ms Thompson, would you like to come to afternoon tea with me?'

'Thank you, m'learned friend, I would,' she said.

'Good. When?' He took his phone out of his pocket and checked his diary. 'This weekend?'

Sammy grabbed her phone to check her diary, too. 'Sorry, I can't. I'm in Somerset doing a shoot with an organic cider producer.'

'OK.' He checked the next week. 'How's Wednesday afternoon looking for you?'

Sammy nodded. 'I've got a planning meeting at one of the magazines in London that morning, so Wednesday afternoon is pretty much perfect for me.'

'Great. I'll book something tomorrow and let you know where and what time,' he said. 'Call me if there's a problem and we'll reschedule if we need to.'

'OK. That sounds good.'

'And I'd better let you get on.' He stood up, and she saw him to the door.

He kissed her goodbye, being careful to keep his libido in check. 'See you on Wednesday,' he said.

And he could hardly wait.

CHAPTER SIX

WEDNESDAY.

A seriously posh hotel.

For afternoon tea.

Panic flooded through Sammy the more she thought about it. Given that kind of venue, she could hardly turn up in her usual black trousers. But a business suit with opaque tights wouldn't be appropriate, either; they were having an Indian summer, even though it was late September. Wearing a floaty cotton dress meant having bare legs or wearing the sheerest tights; and either of those options would mean that the scar on her left leg would be clearly visible.

Even though Nick would probably be too nice to ask her what had caused the scar, she'd know that he was wondering about it. Or maybe he'd recognise it as something that he'd seen before, on his nephew's leg. And in the end she'd cave in and tell him that she'd had a strange bony lump on her shin as a teen, and when it had been investigated the doctors had told her that she had osteosarcoma.

Bone cancer.

Chemotherapy had shrunk the tumour before the operation, and the surgeon had been able to take out the tumour from the bone and put in a metal prosthesis. Sammy knew she'd been one of the lucky ones, able to have bone-sparing surgery rather than an amputation. She'd done every single breathing exercise and every single physiotherapy exercise to the letter after the operation. She'd been through more chemotherapy to mop up any last bad cells after the operation and she'd attended every single one of her regular checkups. And she was hugely grateful that she'd come through it.

She was strong. She had the full support of her family.

And when she'd met Bryn, she'd thought she'd finally found someone different.

But instead he'd gone on to break her heart. He'd asked her to marry him just before she'd had her scare, two years before. And then he'd ended it the day she'd got the results. He'd admitted that he couldn't cope with the prospect of her having cancer again, but he hadn't wanted to be the bad guy who'd dumped the cancer patient. Instead, he'd waited until they knew she was clear—and then he'd dumped her.

Just as well they hadn't actually chosen the engagement ring.

Sammy had walked away with her head held high and her heart feeling as if it had been ground into sand. And she'd promised herself she'd never make the mistake of getting that close to anyone again. Yet, right now, she was taking a huge risk. This would be her third date with Nick—and she didn't have an exit strategy in place.

She dragged in a breath. Nick's nephew had been diagnosed with osteosarcoma, so maybe Nick would understand more than the average person.

But what if he didn't?

What if it made him back away? What if she repulsed him?

Even Bryn—who'd been engaged to her—hadn't coped with her scars. Not really. They'd always made love with the lights off, and he'd been careful never to look at her leg or touch it. She'd pretended that it didn't matter…but it had.

And it mattered now.

She really wasn't ready to tell Nick about her past yet.

She didn't want to call off their date, either; given that she'd already told him how much she liked going out for afternoon tea, she knew he wouldn't believe a feeble excuse. And, being a lawyer, of course he'd ask questions.

Probing ones.

Ones where even a silent reaction would help him to see the truth.

Sammy still hadn't worked out how to deal with the situation by the time she met up with her best friends for a long-planned evening with pizza at her flat.

Except Ashleigh and Claire had known her for long enough to guess that something was wrong.

'Spit it out,' Claire said.

'What?' Sammy asked, feigning innocence.

'You're very quiet. Which isn't you, unless you're concentrating on a shoot. So talk to us,' Ashleigh said. 'That's what best friends are for. To listen, to tell you when you're being an idiot, and to give you a hug when you need one.'

Sammy actually felt tears pricking her eyes

at Ashleigh's words, and was cross with herself for it. For pity's sake. She wasn't one of those people who bawled their eyes out at the drop of a hat.

'Did you find another lump?' Claire asked softly.

'No. Why does everyone *always* assume it's the cancer come back, if something's bothering me?' Sammy asked, losing her cool.

Ashleigh and Claire immediately put down their cutlery, stood up and enveloped her in a hug.

'We're not assuming anything,' Ashleigh said, stroking her hair. 'But we've known you for years, we can see you're upset, and we want to be here for you.'

'It's just something stupid.' Sammy swallowed hard to keep the tears back. She wasn't weak. She was independent and strong. She could do this.

'Then it's something we can help you with—and make you laugh about,' Claire pointed out. 'Don't push us away. There's a fine line between being independent and being too stubborn, you know.'

She and Ashleigh returned to their chairs, but each of them kept hold of one of Sammy's hands.

'I don't know what to wear on a date,' Sammy muttered.

'OK,' Ashleigh said carefully. 'Where are you going, and is it a first date?'

'Afternoon tea at a posh hotel.' Sammy knew this was something she should have told them about before. Because they were her best friends and they had her best interests at heart. They wouldn't judge her. They never had. 'Third date.'

Claire and Ashleigh exchanged a glance. 'Is there going to be a fourth?' Claire asked.

Was she going to break her three-date rule for Nick? 'I don't know.' She wanted to. And she didn't. All at the same time. 'It's driving me crazy,' she admitted.

'Tell us about him,' Ashleigh said.

So Sammy found herself spilling the beans. How she'd taken Nick's photograph for the charity calendar, then ended up having dinner with him—which didn't count as a date, because then that would mean that afternoon tea was the scary fourth—and they'd seen each other a couple of times since.

'Does he know about your leg?' Claire asked.

Sammy shook her head. 'It hasn't been the right time to talk about it, yet.'

'If he's involved with the calendar, he must

have a connection to the ward,' Ashleigh suggested.

'Yes. His nephew had osteosarcoma,' Sammy said.

'So he'll understand,' Ashleigh reassured her. 'If you're even thinking about a fourth date with him, Sammy, it's serious. So you're going to have to tell him.'

'And you have to do it before you end up naked with him and he sees the scar,' Claire added.

Ice slid down Sammy's spine. 'Because you think he'll reject me when he sees it?' That had happened before. A mistake she'd made three times until she'd learned to keep it to herself. Until Bryn, who'd made her trust him…and then let her down even more than the run-for-the-hills boyfriends.

'No, of course not. I mean because when you have sex with him for the first time you want to enjoy it, not worry about having to explain your medical history to him beforehand,' Claire said, rolling her eyes.

'And if you think he's not going to see you for who you are, then you shouldn't be thinking about having sex with him anyway—because in that case he's not good enough for you,' Ashleigh added firmly.

'I know.' Sammy rubbed a hand over her short crop. But even if her hair had been at its longest, she wouldn't have been able to hide behind it because her best friends knew her so well. 'He's a good man—he's ethical and honest.'

'Unlike a certain person I'd like to stake out in a field of fire ants while he was covered in honey,' Claire said darkly. Sammy knew she was referring to Bryn.

'Why can't you wear your usual black trousers, maybe with a top that's a bit more dressy than usual?' Ashleigh asked.

'Because it's the kind of place where I need to wear a dress.'

'Where are you going?' Claire asked.

When Sammy told them the name of the hotel, they both whistled.

'The afternoon tea there is meant to be amazing,' Ashleigh said. 'You have to go and tell us so we can live vicariously through you. Don't chicken out.'

The problem was, Sammy wanted to chicken out. This was the third date. Crunch time. And she knew she was making a fuss about what to wear so she could avoid facing the real reason why she didn't want to go—that she was afraid it would all go wrong and she'd end up hurt again.

'Actually, you can wear a dress, Cinderella. Because your fairy godmother just happened to get some new material delivered last week that would be perfect for you,' Claire said. 'It's purple and I think it's got your name written all over it.'

Her best friend was going to make her a dress, especially for her date? 'Claire-bear, I can't ask you to—' Sammy began.

'You're not asking, I'm offering,' Claire cut in. 'In fact, I'm telling you.'

'If you make me a dress,' Sammy said, 'I'm paying for it, and I don't mean mates' rates.'

'What, like you let me pay you for my wedding photographs and all the shots you took for my website—*not*?' Claire scoffed. 'No. I'm doing it because I want to make you a dress. Just occasionally, Sammy, it's nice to be able to do something as a treat for one of my best friends, OK? So shut up and say yes instead of being over-independent.'

'OK. And sorry. And I really, really appreciate you,' Sammy said.

Claire cuffed her arm playfully. 'So you should, Sammikins. I was thinking an empire line maxi dress, with a V-neck, in two layers—plain underneath and chiffon on top.'

It always amazed Sammy how Claire could see the perfect dress for someone whenever she looked at them. And Claire's creations were stunning. Ashleigh's wedding dress had been amazing.

'You've got heels to go with it?' Claire asked.

'Just because I tend to live in trousers, it doesn't mean I don't own any pretty shoes,' Sammy said.

'Good. Bring them tomorrow night for your fitting so I can make sure the hem's right,' Claire said.

'And what about jewellery?' Ashleigh asked. 'Because Mum had a string of black pearls that'd look fabulous with what Claire's just described. I'll bring them with me tomorrow.'

Sammy had to swallow the lump in her throat. Ashleigh's parents had been killed in a car accident eight years ago, so for Ashleigh to offer to lend her friend something so very precious… 'Thanks.'

'Hey.' Ashleigh hugged her. 'You're worth it.'

'You do know that when you two start having babies, I'll take portraits of the babies every single month for you. As a best friend gift,' Sammy said. The same way she'd done their wedding photographs and had refused to take any payment for even the photographic paper.

'Godmother gift, not just best friend,' Claire corrected. 'And I'm really glad you brought the subject up, because…' She paused for dramatic effect. 'Well, there's something I need to ask you both. Sean agrees with me. Will you both be godmothers?'

Sammy's jaw dropped. 'Oh, my God. You're actually having a baby?'

'In six months' time,' Claire confirmed.

'Oh, that's fantastic.' Sammy hugged her. 'I'm so pleased for you and Sean.'

Ashleigh coughed. 'Seeing as we're doing news, I guess I have a little announcement, too.'

'What?' Sammy stared at her in amazement. 'You and Luke, too?'

'In six months' time, too.' Ashleigh nodded. 'And I'll be looking for you both to be godmothers as well.'

'I'm the only one of us who can drink alcohol now, or I'd rush out and buy a bottle of champagne,' Sammy said. 'Both of you, expecting at the same time. That's *amazing*. Such brilliant news.'

'So, if this thing works out with your barrister, you're absolutely not allowed to get married to him until after we've had the babies,' Claire said, 'because I'm not planning to walk down the aisle behind you in a maternity matron of honour dress.'

'Seconded,' Ashleigh said. 'And we are so drinking champagne at your wedding. Which we can't do when we're pregnant.'

'Two babies,' Sammy said, beaming at both of them. 'That is, I'm assuming neither of you are having twins?'

'Not me,' Claire said.

'Just one baby here, too. But we're waiting until the baby's born to find out if we're having a girl or a boy. Luke and I agreed we wouldn't ask,' Ashleigh said.

'That's fabulous. Really fabulous.' Sammy was thrilled for her friends, she really was.

But at the same time there was a tiny chunk of ice in the middle of her heart.

One of the downsides of having chemotherapy at sixteen was that she'd had to have some eggs frozen in case she wanted to have children when she was older. But there were no guarantees that IVF would work—and she knew that could be a deal-breaker for any potential partner.

Including Nick. She thought about Nick. She had no idea whether he wanted children or not, and she couldn't think of an easy way to ask him. In any case, it was way too early to ask him right now. They'd only been out together twice. So she'd have to add it to the list of difficult conversations they'd need to have if things worked out between them. Cancer, fertility…no wonder her exes had panicked and run. And she was pretty sure that Nick had some issues, too. No way could someone with such a good heart and a keen intellect—perfect partner material—be single at his age without some emotional baggage.

Or maybe she was over-thinking it and she should just treat this whole thing as a chance to have some fun.

Whatever, she knew that she had to tell him the truth about herself.

But not just yet…

The following evening, Sammy met her best friends at Claire's shop for the dress fitting. She put on the high heels she planned to wear with the dress, and Claire adjusted the hem.

'You look a million dollars,' Ashleigh said, and looped the black pearls round Sammy's neck.

'Totally stunning,' Claire agreed. 'Your barrister isn't going to know what hit him.'

And there wasn't a single inch of leg displayed above Sammy's ankle. The dress was floaty, feminine and gorgeous, and Sammy didn't quite recognise herself in the mirror.

'Thank you. Both of you.' The lump in her throat made her voice all croaky.

'Hey. We want to see you as happy as we are,' Ashleigh said softly. 'Which doesn't mean we're trying to marry you off—you don't have to be married to be happy. But I know you've been lonely since Bryn.'

'Hey. I have a brilliant family and the best friends I could ask for,' Sammy said. 'Asking for more is greedy.'

'No, it's not,' Claire said. 'You deserve it. Enjoy your date.'

So what would his mysterious Woman in Black be wearing today? Nick wondered. Something dressy, given their surroundings. But he was pretty sure it would be black.

As he became aware of someone entering the room, he looked up from checking the emails on his phone and did a double take.

Not black, then.

And very, *very* dressy.

He'd never have believed that Sammy scrubbed up so well. She took his breath away. She was wearing only the lightest make-up, but that dress…

He stood up when she walked over to their table. 'You look amazing,' he said.

She blushed. 'Thank you.'

'Really amazing,' he said, sitting down again after the waiter had seated her.

'And note that I'm not wearing black,' she said with a self-deprecating smile.

He smiled. 'I'd guessed that you'd wear a little black dress. I'm glad I was wrong.'

'I did tell you that my best friend's a dress designer. And she's amazingly talented.'

'I'll second that,' he said.

The waiter ran through the list of teas. 'I'd recommend one of the black or green teas with the sandwiches and savouries,' he said, 'and then a fruit infusion with the sweet selection.'

'That sounds perfect,' Sammy said. 'Could I have Earl Grey, please?'

'And for me, too,' Nick said.

'I've never been here,' she said when the waiter had gone. 'Claire and Ash—my best friends—would love this. It's like a proper Regency drawing room. And there's even a pianist.'

Nick raised an eyebrow. 'He could be playing this one especially for you right now.'

'Debussy's "Girl with the Flaxen Hair".' She smiled back. 'Maybe.'

'Not a fan of Debussy?' he asked.

'Beethoven all the way for me,' Sammy said.

Romantic. Why didn't that surprise him?

The waiter brought over their tea in a silver pot, and a sage-and-cream striped porcelain tray to match their cups, saucers and tea plates, filled with a selection of sandwiches and savouries.

'I'm really glad I skipped lunch,' Sammy said. 'I don't know where to start. The sandwiches—smoked salmon, roast beef, ham, or cucumber and cream cheese?'

'I'd say the Welsh rarebit first, as it's hot,' Nick suggested. 'Then maybe we should start at one end of the tray of sandwiches and work our way through.'

'Great idea. This is such a treat. Thank you so much for inviting me.'

'I can't think of anyone I'd rather share this with,' Nick said. And he realised how true it was. He enjoyed Sammy's company hugely. Strange that this was only their third official date. It felt as if he'd known her for years and years. He was comfortable with her, felt that he could be himself—and that was such a rare feeling. Something that made him want to take things a lot further between them. Because maybe Sammy was the one he could learn to trust. The one who'd help to mend his heart again.

Once they'd finished the savoury platter, he excused himself and had a quiet word with the pianist.

When the waiter brought the fruit teas—lemon verbena for him and strawberry and rhubarb for Sammy—with the three-tiered cake stand containing the sweet selection, Sammy looked at Nick with slightly narrowed eyes. 'Did you just say something to the pianist?'

'I might've done,' he said, lifting one shoulder in a shrug.

'The Moonlight Sonata is my favourite piece of music in the world,' she said softly. 'And it's perfect right now. Perfect music, perfect food—and perfect company.'

His thoughts entirely. He gave her a tiny bow. 'Why, thank you, ma'am.'

They made short work of the scones with clotted cream and jam, the lavender shortbread and the tiny rich selection of pastries.

'Oh, yes—a verrine,' Sammy said, looking at the shot glass filled with panna cotta. 'I love it when I get a commission in Paris. It means I get the chance to go to a certain patisserie and have one of their deconstructed desserts.'

'Want to swap mine for your super-chocolatey brownie?' he asked.

She blinked. 'You remembered that I don't like chocolate cake?'

'Of course.' Why was she so surprised? Or maybe she'd just dated the wrong kind of man in the past. Someone who was selfish and never put her first. That would explain why she was single: dating someone selfish would definitely put you off relationships. Naomi had put him off relationships just as badly.

'I've really enjoyed this,' she said when they'd finished. 'Though I don't think I'm going to eat again for a week!'

'Agreed. Though could I tempt you to a glass of wine back at my place?' he asked.

She smiled. 'I'd like that.'

He ordered a taxi to take them back to his flat.

Nick already had half a dozen bottles of his favourite white wines chilling in his wine cooler; he swiftly opened one and poured them both a glass.

'This is lovely,' Sammy said when she'd taken a sip. 'What is it?'

'Montrachet,' he explained. 'It's one of the grand cru chardonnays.'

'It's gorgeous. Really smooth.'

He hooked up his phone to his stereo system, and set some Beethoven piano music playing. And when Sammy put her wine glass on the low coffee table, she ended up curled against him on the sofa, with her head resting on his shoulder.

They didn't even have to talk; and it felt so good, just being together. She felt more relaxed with Nick than she ever had with anyone else—even in the early days with Bryn, before he'd killed her love stone dead and broken her heart.

She knew she ought to tell Nick about her past and explain about her leg; but she just couldn't find the right words, and she didn't want to spoil what had been such a perfect afternoon.

She reached up to trace the curve of his mouth with a forefinger. 'I really enjoyed today.'

'Me, too,' he said.

Even though she knew it was being greedy, wanting something she couldn't have, she couldn't resist stealing a kiss. He responded instantly, wrapping his arms tightly round her and kissing her back.

Everything about this man felt right.

But the fear was still there. Would she repulse

him? When push came to shove, would he too think she wasn't enough of a woman for him?

'Nick, I really have to go,' she said softly. 'I've got a train to Edinburgh at the crack of dawn tomorrow, and it's a four-and-a-half-hour journey.'

'Can I drive you home? I've only had one glass of wine, so I'm below the limit for driving. And yes, I know you're perfectly capable of taking the Tube,' he added swiftly, 'but you're wearing high heels and that gorgeous dress and it won't be much fun keeping the hem out of the way on the escalators.'

True. And she liked the way he was thinking of her. 'Thank you. That would be nice,' she said. Plus it meant she got to spend just a little bit more time with him.

'So what are you doing in Edinburgh?' he asked as he drove her home.

'I'm taking a portrait of a sculptor for one of the Sunday magazines. Actually, it's someone whose work I've admired for a while, so I'm really looking forward to meeting him,' she said. 'What about you?'

'Preparing for a trial which starts next week and might go on for a fortnight or so. How long are you away for?'

'Three days,' she said. 'Shall I call you when

I get back?' And maybe on that long train journey she'd find the right words to tell him about her leg. And, if they managed to negotiate that and come out the other side in one piece, maybe they could do Date Four. Take another step towards a real relationship.

'I'd like that,' he said. He parked outside her flat. 'And I'm guessing you have to pack, check over your equipment and charge up various batteries.'

'Something like that,' she said.

'Then I won't ask to come in for coffee.' He cupped her face in his hand and kissed her goodnight so sweetly that she felt the tears prick her eyelids. 'Sleep well,' he said softly.

'You too,' she said, and stole a last kiss before climbing out of his car.

There was a message on her phone when she got up the next morning. Short, sweet and to the point: *Safe journey.*

Have a good day in chambers, she typed back.

She could really get used to dating Nick Kennedy.

But before she got too comfortable she really had to tell him the truth about herself…

CHAPTER SEVEN

WHILE SAMMY WAS in Edinburgh, she had a chance to explore some of the shoreline of the Firth of Forth; the sculptor whose photograph she was taking was inspired by it, and took her and Ben, the journalist, for a short drive from the city down to Yellowcraigs. They headed off the beaten track, down through a pretty village to the parking area, and then walked out to the beach.

The long, sweeping cove was beautiful. 'I love this sky. I could take your picture here,' Sammy suggested.

'Or on Fidra.' Jimmy McBain pointed to the island. 'I thought we could get a boat over there this morning.'

'Sounds good to me.' Sammy smiled at the journalist. 'OK with you, Ben?'

'I'm not the world's best sailor,' the journalist admitted, 'but I'll give it a go.'

'Just as well I told you to bring your walking boots in a plastic bag,' Jimmy said with a grin. 'And we'll cheer you up when we get back with a wee dram.'

Sammy took a few shots of Jimmy on the beach while he chatted to them about the area.

'So why is the name Fidra familiar?' Ben asked.

Sammy knew the answer to that one. 'Robert Louis Stevenson spent his holidays there as a boy.' When Ben still looked puzzled, she said, 'Pieces of eight? Long John Silver?'

'Oh—*Treasure Island*.'

'That's the one,' Jimmy said, looking pleased. Sammy took a few more shots of the cove while Jimmy was talking to the skipper of a boat, and she thought of Nick and his misty shoreline painting. He'd love it here, she was sure. On impulse, she took a snap of the island on her phone and sent it to him.

Guess where I am?

Clearly he was in chambers rather than in court, because he answered straight away.

I thought you said you were going to Edinburgh?

I did. We're half an hour or so's drive away. This is the island of Fidra.

Fidra?

She smiled.

Tsk. You must've read Treasure Island when you were a kid?

That's Treasure Island?

Jimmy the Sculptor says that's what inspired Robert Louis Stevenson. I think you'd like it here. Ice creams, cafes, miles of sand, and apparently just down the road is biggest colony of puffins on the east coast.

Sounds great, was the response.

Had they been dating long enough to think about going away together? She typed, Wish you were here, then stopped herself. She did wish that she were sharing this with Nick, but was telling him a step too far? She went to delete the message but accidentally pressed the wrong button and sent it instead.

Oh, no.

This time, there was no reply.

Well, it served her right for being way too forward. Of course it was too soon to think about going away together. How ridiculous of her to think otherwise.

Thankfully right then they had to get on the boat, and after that her time was caught up taking photographs, so it stopped her brooding about the situation.

Then her phone beeped on their way back to the city.

Sorry about earlier. I was called back to court so my phone was off. Wish I was there, too.

It made Sammy feel all warm inside.

And it clearly showed on her face, because Jimmy patted her arm. 'Message from your man, was it?'

'Yes.'

'He's a lucky lad. You'd have plenty of admirers up here, even though your haircut's… well.' He rolled his eyes. 'You'd be a bonnier lass if you'd let it grow.'

She smiled back. 'It's short right now because I donate my hair to make wigs for children who've had cancer.'

Jimmy whistled. 'So you've a good heart, too. That's rare. Bonny, and with a good heart.'

'And it'd make a great story,' Ben said, looking interested.

'Agreed. I can get you some people to interview, if you like,' Sammy said. 'Especially as I happened to shoot a calendar which is going to raise money for the cancer ward. You could maybe do an article on that. Hot men stripping off to raise money.'

'It'd be a good human interest story.' Ben held her gaze. 'And I can start by interviewing you.'

She shook her head. 'I'd rather stay behind the lens.'

He could see that she meant it and he left it there rather than nagging, but Sammy found herself thinking about it on the way back to London, the next morning. Maybe if she went public about her experience, it would help someone else to get through their own situation. And talking to Ben about it might be a good test run, something that would give her the courage to talk to Nick.

'Ben—did you mean it about that interview?' she asked.

'Which one?' He groaned. 'Sorry. My brain is totally scrambled. Never let me agree to drink with a Scots guy again.'

'Or a cider producer in Somerset—I'm sure

you had a hangover after that interview, too,' she said with a grin. 'I mean the article about the charity calendar and why I donate my hair.'

'Yes, I meant it. Though give me a while for my brain to unscramble so I can work up some decent questions.'

'Sure. I'll get you a cup of tea and a bacon sandwich from the buffet.' And she'd better hope that her courage didn't fail her in the time between now and when her colleague had recovered from his hangover.

It didn't. And Ben was incredibly kind with his questions.

'I had no idea that you'd been through all that,' he said when he'd finished the interview.

'I don't talk about it because I don't want cancer to define me,' she said simply.

He nodded. 'I admired you before, because you're always so professional and you deliver every single time. But knowing you had to cope with all that as well—you're really amazing, Sammy.'

'That isn't why I told you. It's not about my ego. I want to give other people some hope so they know you really can come out the other side of the experience and it'll be OK,' she said. 'Though is there any way you can do the piece without actually revealing who I am?'

He raised an eyebrow. 'You think people might not want to hire you because you're a cancer survivor?'

'Some people don't react so well,' she said. Personally as well as professionally. Not that she wanted to explain that.

Ben gave her a pithy response about precisely what that kind of people could do.

'I still have to earn my living,' she said.

'I'll talk to my editor and see if we can find a way round it,' he said. 'But thank you. Now I know your story—well, I'm really proud to call myself your colleague.'

'And friend,' she said. 'Now shut up before I start being wet.'

He grinned. 'That's the last word I'd ever use to describe you.'

Talking to Ben had been so easy.

But was that simply because he was a journalist, used to asking questions and teasing the real story out of reluctant interviewees? Would it be as easy, talking to Nick?

Ben was her colleague. Her friend. She'd known him for years. There was no way that her past could change their relationship.

Whereas Nick was…

Help.

Not her lover. Not yet. Though she wanted him to be. 'Boyfriend' sounded twee. Partner? They hadn't been together that long. But she really felt she'd clicked with him. While she'd been away in Edinburgh, she'd really missed him, and it had shocked her how much she'd wanted to share all her new experiences with him. Had he missed her? Or had he been so busy that he'd barely registered her absence?

She was probably over-thinking things again.

Why couldn't she be like she was in every other area of her life? Why couldn't she just step up and do it? Tell him?

'You are such a coward, Samantha Jane Thompson,' she told herself grimly.

Back at her flat, she found a rectangular parcel waiting for her. It had fitted perfectly through her letterbox, and she recognised the box as one from a very exclusive chocolatier.

There was a note with it in bold script that was clearly from a fountain pen:

Welcome home. Missed you.

So he *had* missed her as much as she'd missed him. And what a welcome home. She hardly knew where to start when she opened the box; they were glorious, and each one was a treat. Best of all was the dark chocolate violet crème.

She glanced at her watch. It was a Saturday, but Nick had said that he was preparing for a trial. He was probably knee-deep in paperwork. Better not to disturb him, then. She texted him instead of calling.

Thank you so much for the chocolates. They're sublime. Might not be any left by the time I see you! *insert guilty smiley*

When he didn't reply, she knew that her guess about him being really busy was right. But, to her surprise, he called her at half past five.

'Hey. So did you find any treasure on your island?'

'I took some good shots, if that counts.' She laughed. 'And thank you for the chocolates. They're amazing. Though, um, there aren't many left to share with you.'

'My pleasure. Besides, they're meant for you, not for sharing.' His voice was full of warmth. 'I just wanted to welcome you back.'

And how. Which gave her the courage to

suggest Date Four. Something she hadn't done in a long, long time. 'Are you busy tonight, or do you want to do something?'

'Aren't you tired after that long train journey?' he asked.

'A bit,' she admitted, 'but if you're not busy maybe we could have a quick drink or something.'

'I really missed you,' he said softly. 'How about we compromise and I'll come over to you with a takeaway?'

She'd been away for three days so she hadn't had a chance to restock her fridge, apart from the carton of milk she'd grabbed at the train station. She padded over to it and glanced inside. 'It seems I have a bottle of Prosecco in the fridge,' she said. She opened the freezer door. 'And some posh ice cream.'

'Perfect. I'll order something to be delivered to yours and be with you at seven.'

'Sounds good to me.'

At precisely seven, her doorbell rang. She opened the door and greeted Nick with a hug. 'Hey.' Then she stepped back and took in his appearance; he was wearing an expensively cut wool suit, a handmade white shirt and an understated silk tie.

'I feel very scruffy compared with you,' she said. 'I wish now I'd changed.'

'Instead of working?' He smiled. 'You had a long journey and it was sensible to dress for comfort.'

'I can change now.'

'Too late. Dinner's just arrived,' he said, indicating the white van emblazoned with the name of a Thai restaurant that had pulled up outside her flat. 'Perfect timing, too.'

Over dinner, she showed him some of the shots of Fidra.

'That beach looks amazing,' he said.

'It's gorgeous. That sweeping cove…'

'Maybe,' he said, 'we could go there together sometime.'

Maybe. If he still wanted to know her, once she'd told him about her past.

But for a workaholic like Nick to suggest taking some time away… 'I'd like that,' she said.

They ended up stretched out on her sofa, all warm and smoochy. Sammy's legs were entangled with his, his hands were flat against her back underneath her T-shirt—and how good his skin felt against hers—and her arms were wrapped round his neck.

It would be oh, so easy to suggest that they moved from her sofa to her bed, where they could shut the world away. Where they could take the time to explore each other, discover where each other liked being touched and kissed.

Except...she still hadn't told him.

And letting him find out by seeing her scar—or, worse, touching it by accident—would be totally wrong.

'Sammy? Is everything OK?'

Clearly he'd picked up on her tension.

'Just tired,' she fibbed. 'It's been a long few days with a lot of travelling.'

Nick kissed her gently. 'I'd better go and let you get some sleep.'

Now. Tell him now. Don't be such a coward. He's not going to run for the hills. He's not going to react the way Bryn and the others did.

'Sorry,' she said, chickening out.

'It's fine. I'll call you tomorrow.' He gave her a last lingering kiss. 'I'll see myself out. Sweet dreams.'

And, even though she was tired, she couldn't sleep. She lay there in the dark, regretting her cowardice. Why was it so hard to tell him the truth?

Over the next couple of weeks, Sammy and Nick spent as much time together as they could. The more she got to know him, the more she liked him, and she hoped it might be the same for him. They had similar tastes in music; they both liked complicated whodunnit dramas—though he always made some comment about the legal bits being wrong—and they both liked outrageous stand-up comedy and long walks on the beach and browsing through little art galleries.

This could be perfect. With Nick, she felt as if she really fitted.

All she had to do was tell him.

The truth, the whole truth and nothing but the truth.

How hard could it be?

She even practised it in front of the mirror. *Nick, there's something I need to tell you. I'll understand if you want to call the whole thing off, but fourteen years ago I had...*

Six letters.

Two syllables.

A word that could explode someone's whole world and leave nothing but rubble.

Three dates on the trot, she tried to tell him—and failed.

Then he said to her, 'On Saturday, Mandy's going on a spa day with a couple of her friends—it's a birthday present from them. I promised her I'd look after the boys for her.' He paused. 'I was wondering, would you like to spend the day with us?'

He wanted her to meet his family?

This was serious.

And this was his nephew who'd had osteosarcoma.

Oh, help. She really, really needed to tell him about her past, but she still hadn't found the right time or the right words to tell him.

There was a wary look in his eyes; clearly he was half expecting her to refuse. It would probably be sensible to refuse, yet at the same time she didn't want to hurt him. How could she throw the offer back in his face? She had a feeling this wasn't the kind of thing he suggested very often.

'Actually,' she said, 'I like kids very much. I have two nieces and two nephews myself, and my family's really close. How old are the boys?'

'Xander's twelve and Ned's eight.'

'Good ages,' she said. Stupid. Any age was a good age. 'My nephews are very slightly older.' And now she was babbling. Focus, Sammy, she told herself. 'Maybe we could go to the park if it's a nice day, or somewhere like the Natural History Museum if it's wet.'

'That's a great idea,' he said. 'I'll pick you up.'

Tell him. Tell him now.

'Nick…'

'Yes?'

For a split second, she glimpsed vulnerability in his face.

No, she couldn't tell him right now.

'What?' he asked.

She thought on her feet. 'Please don't think I'm being nosey here, but I just need to know if there are any topics of conversation I ought to steer clear of on Saturday?'

He nodded. 'Xander's a bit sensitive about his leg. And we don't talk about their father.'

She winced inwardly. 'I take it from that, he let them down?'

'Big time,' he said, his face tightening. 'Mandy doesn't want anyone to badmouth him in front of the boys, in case he ever decides to come back into their lives, but…' He looked grim. 'I can't ever see that happening. Warren the Weasel walked out on them the day they got Xander's diagnosis, eighteen months ago, and they haven't seen him since.'

Sammy sucked in a breath, shocked beyond measure. She could just about get her head round the reasons why someone might not be able to cope with their partner's diagnosis and walk away, but to do something like that to their child… 'That's pretty rough on your sister and the boys.'

'Yeah.' His lip curled. 'Warren's the most selfish man I've ever met. He hasn't even sent the boys a birthday or Christmas card since he left. Mandy's been trying to keep the lines of communication open and she takes them to see his parents. Warren's mother always makes excuses for him, saying he's "sensitive"—' Nick made exaggerated quote marks with his fingers as he said the words '—but he's certainly not sensitive to his sons' feelings. Or to his ex-wife's. The only people he cares about are me, myself and I.' He blew out a breath. 'Thankfully Mandy had the sense to divorce him for unreasonable behaviour, and he had the sense not to dispute it.'

With a hotshot barrister as an ex-brother-in-law, Warren would have been very stupid indeed to try to contest a divorce petition, Sammy thought. And it sounded as if Nick seriously disliked the man.

'I'm sorry,' she said.

Nick shrugged. 'It's not your fault.'

'I know, but still a horrible situation for you all to deal with.' She took a deep breath. 'And that's empathy speaking, not pity.' She'd had enough pity after her diagnosis to last a lifetime; no way would she ever give pity to someone else.

He drew her into his arms and held her close. 'Thank you. It's appreciated.' He sighed and brushed his mouth against her hair. 'We're not very good at marriage in my family.'

So was this the reason why he was single? Because he'd been so badly bitten that he didn't want to risk falling in love again? Not sure what to say, she stroked his face.

'Sorry. I shouldn't burden you with my woes,' he said, looking guilty.

'No, that's fine. And it's not going any further than me.'

He kissed her lightly. 'I know. And thanks. Again.' He grimaced. 'I guess you ought to know what you're getting yourself into. My parents split up when I was seventeen. My sister—well, I've told you about the weasel she married. And I'm divorced as well. So we're not a good bet, the Kennedys.'

'Or maybe you haven't met the right person for you yet.' She worked it out. He would've been in the middle of his exams when his parents split up. A really vulnerable, impressionable time.

'Maybe,' he said. 'Dad kind of buried himself in work after my mother left.'

Not 'Mum', she noticed. It sounded as if he wasn't close to his mother. Did he blame her for the divorce? But asking felt too much like prying.

'Do you see much of your parents?' she asked carefully.

'Dad lives in Brussels, so we don't see him that often.' He gave her a rueful smile. 'He specialises in European law. I guess he hoped I'd follow in his footsteps, but I like London too much.'

'What about your mother?'

He shrugged. 'She's even further away, in Cornwall.'

She frowned. 'How can Cornwall be further away from London than Brussels?'

'It's quicker to get the Eurostar to Brussels than to drive to the far depths of Cornwall,' he said.

She had a feeling that there was a bit more to it than that, but pushing would be unfair. 'So they don't get to see much of their grandchildren, then?'

'No. Which is a shame, because Mandy could've done with their support after Warren left. Dad's very busy in Brussels, and our mother has her B&B to think about. But Mandy knows she can always rely on me, even though I'm the baby of the family.' He smiled. 'And it's not a burden—not at all. Xander and Ned are nice kids. Plus it means I have a cast-iron excuse to see all the superhero films at the cinema, because I can take them.'

'Sounds good. I do something similar with my nephews and nieces,' she said lightly.

Guilt seeped through her. Nick had been open with her. She really ought to tell him what he was getting into, too. The spectre of cancer, fertility issues, the fact she wasn't really a whole woman…the Sammy Thompson he'd met was a fake.

But the words dried up in her throat when she tried to utter them.

She'd tell him.

Soon.

And was it so wrong to want to feel like a normal person without complications for just that little bit longer, instead of turning into Sammy-the-cancer-survivor?

CHAPTER EIGHT

SATURDAY DAWNED BRIGHT and sunny. Although it was the beginning of October it was still really warm.

Nick called Sammy's landline. 'We're outside in the car,' he said.

'Great. I'm coming out to join you,' she told him.

To her secret amusement, although he was wearing jeans he was also wearing another of those white handmade shirts; she guessed he was always going to have that touch of formality.

The boys were both sitting in the back of the car. Sammy could see the family resemblance to Nick in their dark hair and dark eyes. She was curious as to how he was going to introduce her to them: as his friend or as his girlfriend?

'Boys, this is my friend Sammy,' he said.

'Sammy, these are my nephews, Xander and Ned.'

Friend, then—which was sensible. Especially given the situation with their father; Nick obviously wouldn't want to introduce the boys to a string of 'aunties', feeling that they'd had enough change in their life already. She could understand that.

The boys chorused hello, both looking slightly shy.

Sammy smiled at them. 'It's very nice to meet you both. Nick says we're going to the park—is that OK with you?'

Ned looked thrilled. 'They have a really cool zip-wire at the park.'

'That sounds like fun,' she said. 'Are adults allowed on it?'

'You like zip-wires?' Ned asked, his eyes round with surprise.

'I love them,' she said. 'Race you?'

'You're on,' Ned said with a grin.

Nick drove them to a park that the boys clearly knew well. There was a play area with a massive slide wide enough to take four people at a time and a low zip-wire, and the boys spent most of their time there. Sammy raced Nick down the slide and joined the boys on the zip-wire.

Then she noticed a stall selling water pistols and nudged Nick. 'My brothers, sister and I loved that sort of thing when I was a kid. I bet the boys will, too.'

He raised his eyebrows. 'You're challenging us to a water fight?'

'Ah, no. I was thinking me and the boys versus you.'

'Three against one? That's totally unfair.' But he was laughing, so she was pretty sure he was up for it. 'Where are we going to get water from?' he asked.

She gestured to the kiosk at the other side of the playing field. 'I'm pretty sure they'll sell bottled water. That'll do the job.'

'Hmm.'

'Ned, Xander—team huddle,' she said, beckoning the boys over.

'Team huddle?' they asked, mystified, but went with her.

'Water fight. Us versus Uncle Nick,' she explained economically. 'What do you think?'

'Yeah,' they chorused, each pumping a fist into the air.

She bought four water pistols and two large bottles of still water, and she enjoyed charging round with the boys and doing her best to soak Nick with water. Though she noticed that

Xander was looking tired at almost the same time as Nick clearly did, because Nick stopped dead and said, 'Right, time for a truce.'

'Not a chance,' she said.

He came over to her and lowered his voice. 'They've been running around like mad and Xander's in danger of overdoing it. He needs to rest.'

She murmured back, 'I know. Trust me.' Then she turned to Xander. 'I've been thinking—with three of us, we're getting in each other's way. I reckon we need a master strategist to direct us, and I think out of the three of us you'd be the best one to do that.'

The boy looked slightly suspicious. 'Master strategist? Really?'

'Really,' she confirmed. 'Come and sit down here by this tree so you've got the best view of the field. Now, imagine you're the shepherd, Ned and I are the sheepdogs, and Uncle Nick's the big fat sheep who's about to get a bath.'

'And?'

'So you need to direct us,' she said. 'And if you do it right, then we win and your Uncle Nick gets totally soaked.'

Xander stopped looking suspicious and grinned. 'Let's do it.'

She and Ned followed Xander's shouted directions, and finally managed to soak Nick from head to foot.

'OK, I surrender,' Nick said, laughing.

And, with that white shirt and his jeans plastered to his skin so the outline of his pectorals and gluteus maximus were perfectly defined, he looked utterly gorgeous. Sammy had already noticed how many female heads he was turning during the water fight, and several more seemed to be showing interest in a hot, wet man.

'We won, Sammy!' Ned crowed. He rushed over to her and hugged her.

'That's because we had a great strategy director,' she said, and high-fived Xander and then Ned, who both beamed at her.

'Not that brilliant,' Nick said calmly. Before Sammy realised what he was planning to do, he'd picked up all four water pistols and soaked her. 'Revenge,' he said with a grin, 'is sweet.'

'Oh, you monster—you'd already surrendered so that's totally cheating,' she said, laughing. 'For that you can buy me an ice cream, and I'm going to sit down here and get Xander to protect me.' She took one of the water pistols from Nick, refilled it, and handed it to Xander. 'You're my bodyguard.'

'Cool,' Xander said.

'Can we have ice creams, too? A whippy one with a chocolate flake?' Ned asked hopefully, adding belatedly, 'Please?'

'Whippy ice cream with a chocolate flake—is there any other kind?' Sammy teased.

'Hint taken.' Nick rolled his eyes. 'Come on, Ned. Let's go and queue up.'

Xander had gone quiet, she noticed. 'Are you OK?' she asked softly when Nick and Ned had left.

The boy sighed. 'I just wish… I hate my stupid leg. I know you're just being nice about letting me rest.'

'Hey. We needed you as our strategy director,' she said. 'And now to protect me against sneaky water attacks from Nick.'

'I'm twelve, not a baby like Ned—I knew what you were doing. But my leg had started hurting a bit so I went along with it.' Then he glanced at her. 'Sorry, Uncle Nick and Mum would be mad at me for being rude to you.'

'You're not being rude, just honest—and if your leg starts aching of course it's going to make you feel fed up and grumpy.'

'It aches nearly all the time,' Xander said

with a sigh. 'They had to take part of my bone away, so there's a metal thing in my leg they have to expand when the rest of my bones grow.'

'Meaning you don't have to have lots of operations, just the one? That's really good,' she said.

He blinked at her. 'Uncle Nick says you know someone who had what I did. That's why you photographed him and everyone else for the calendar.'

'I do.' She paused. This was a huge risk—but it might help the boy to feel a bit happier. 'Want to know a secret?'

'What sort of secret?'

'A really, really big secret. But you have to promise not to tell anyone,' she warned.

'Cross my heart and hope to die,' he said, making the sign of a cross over his heart with his fingertip.

Sammy glanced over towards Nick. He and Ned were in the queue at the ice cream van so they probably couldn't see, but even so she shifted so she could hide her legs from Nick's view in case he turned round, and pushed up the left leg of her jeans to her knee.

Xander's eyes went wide. 'You've got a scar in the same place as me.'

'Yes, and for exactly the same reason,' she said softly. 'But I was a little bit older than you—I was sixteen when I had my op.'

'Did it hurt?'

'My leg?' At his nod, she said softly, 'After the op, yes.'

'Does it hurt now?'

'No.'

'And you had to have more than one op?'

'Luckily not, because I'd pretty much stopped growing at sixteen—but some of my friends did.' She swallowed hard. 'This is your and my secret, Xander, OK?'

'OK,' Xander said.

'Good. And it's important to do your exercises, even when they're boring and even when they hurt a little bit.'

'Why?' he asked.

'Because it means you get strong,' she said. 'And, next time you think you can't do something and your leg's holding you back, remember that I go all over the world in my job. It doesn't hold me back.'

'Have you been to Australia?' he challenged.

'And America, and Japan.' She paused. 'And I climbed Mount Kilimanjaro three years ago.'

His eyes went wide. 'Really? You climbed a mountain? Even after…you know?'

'Yup. I can show you the photographs. I went as the team photographer, but obviously I had to go where they went, so that meant climbing with them.'

He looked impressed. 'That's *so* cool.'

'I know. Though I guess I should admit that it isn't the climb that's the hard thing—it's not like rock-climbing where you see people sticking an axe into the cliff or what have you and hauling themselves up. It's the altitude that makes it difficult. The air's really thin, so you have to walk incredibly slowly or you can't breathe and get dizzy. And sleeping on the hard ground for five or six nights really makes you ache all over. But it was worth it. The views were amazing.' She high-fived him. 'And if I can do anything I like after having osteosarcoma, then so can you. Never, ever let your cancer define you. Because you're more than that.'

For a second, his eyes glistened with tears, but he blinked them away. 'Thanks, Sammy.' His voice was a little hoarse.

'Any time,' she said. 'And any time you want to talk to me, you can—I'll keep whatever you tell me confidential. Uncle Nick's got my phone and email.'

'Thanks—it's really nice having someone who understands.'

Sammy had the strongest feeling that he wanted to tell her something. So she waited, knowing from experience as a photographer that people always filled a silence if you gave them the time.

And he did.

'Uncle Nick always makes me stop and rest before I'm really ready.'

'It's because he loves you,' she said gently, 'and he worries about you, and he's scared you'll overdo it and give yourself a setback.' Just what her family had said to her, when she'd finally lost her temper with everyone and yelled about how being wrapped in cotton wool drove her crazy.

'But I won't overdo it—I'm *twelve*, not stupid.'

'He knows that,' she said, 'but sometimes when you love someone and you're scared for them, that kind of stops you thinking straight.'

'So what do I do?'

'Tell him,' she said simply, knowing that she was the biggest hypocrite in the world—

because she hadn't told Nick what he really ought to know, had she? 'Sit down with him and tell him what you told me. Tell him you're doing all your exercises and you want to get strong, so you're not going to overdo it because you know that'll mean you have to wait even longer before you're fully recovered. Promise him you'll always say when you're tired or you've had enough, and then he'll relax a bit.'

'Is that what you did?'

'Eventually. After a big fight.' And even now she knew she sometimes overdid the independence bit, but she couldn't help it.

Xander nodded. 'I love Uncle Nick. He's a better dad to me than…' He dragged in a breath. 'I'm not supposed to talk about that, either.'

'That your dad left?'

He nodded. 'I hate him. He left us when Mum really needed him. She still cries when she doesn't think I can hear her. I used to think it was my fault for getting sick, but Uncle Nick said it wasn't that at all. I once heard him call my dad a—well, he's right, but Mum would kill me if I used that word.'

Sammy's heart bled for him. She still couldn't get her head round how anyone could be so selfish as to put themselves before their child, especially when their child really needed them. She gave him a hug. 'Xander, if I had a magic wand, I'd fix this—but people are complicated. Maybe your dad was just really scared.'

'Uncle Nick's scared. Mum's scared. Ned's scared. But they didn't leave.' He lifted his head. 'Did your dad leave you when you got cancer?'

'Nope. But some of my boyfriends did.'

'Because they were scared?'

'Something like that.'

'Then they were weasels and you deserve better,' Xander said. 'That's what Uncle Nick says about Dad to Mum.'

'When he thinks you can't hear?'

The boy nodded. 'And because she'd yell at him for using the other word.'

She ruffled his hair. 'I take it they don't know you have ears like a bat, then.'

Xander smiled. 'No. I sometimes think I'd like to be Batman, though.'

'You and me both. Though I'd rather be the Black Widow.'

'In the Avengers? Yeah. She's awesome.'

They were still laughing when Nick and Ned came back with the ice creams.

'What's so funny?' Nick asked.

'We're talking about superhero movies,' Sammy said.

'Sammy wants to be the Black Widow,' Xander informed him.

Nick stood so that the boys couldn't see him and mouthed, 'That works for me—she's hot.'

Sammy had a hard time keeping a straight face and dealing with the rush of heat that went through her.

'I want to be Spiderman,' Ned said.

'And I'm Batman,' Xander said. 'Who would you be, Uncle Nick?'

He sighed. 'You've already bagsied both my favourites.'

'You can be Robin,' Xander said kindly.

Nick shook his head. 'No. I think I'll be Iron Man.'

Sammy shifted so that only Nick could see her face, caught his eye, and mouthed, 'Works for me—*he's* hot.' She had the satisfaction of seeing colour slash across Nick's cheeks. Yeah. Two could play at that game.

And she pushed away the fact that she still hadn't told him the truth.

They went to a fried chicken place for lunch on the way home. Nick turned to Sammy when the boys were out of earshot.

'Thank you—you found a nice way to make Xander rest and not feel that he was missing out. And I apologise. I thought at first you were pushing him too hard.'

She nodded grimly. 'A word to the wise—don't wrap him in cotton wool, because he'll resent it later. You need to find a way of keeping him right in the middle of things and yet resting at the same time.'

'That sounds like experience talking.'

'Uh-huh.' She certainly couldn't tell him what Xander had confided in her, as she'd promised to keep it to herself.

'Would this be your sister who was wrapped in cotton wool?' Nick asked softly.

No, it had been her, for the first week. But, after that huge fight, Sammy's family had learned to support her instead of smothering her. Most of the time. She knew they still panicked, which was why she didn't always tell them if she felt any kind of twinge in her leg. 'I'd rather not talk about it,' she said.

'Your sister's not...?' He stopped and winced. 'I'm sorry. I didn't mean to rip the top off your scars.'

'My sister's fine. Now let's change the subject. I'm sorry for soaking you.'

'I got my own back.'

'Yeah, and your car's a bit soggy.'

'It'll dry,' he said. 'Thank you. You're good with the boys.'

'I'm an aunt of four,' she reminded him, 'so I jolly well ought to be good with kids by now.' She pushed back the surge of longing. She had to be realistic and recognise that she might have to content herself with being an aunt or a godmother. But she'd deal with it when she had to.

'My ex wasn't good with kids,' he said. 'She never really enjoyed spending time with the boys.'

Because she wanted kids of her own and his attention had been focused on them? Sammy wondered. 'That's a shame,' she said.

He gave her a thin smile. 'Yeah. There wasn't a maternal bone in Naomi's body.'

Ah. So she'd got it wrong and Nick's ex hadn't wanted kids. And it sounded as if it had been an issue between them. Maybe one of the issues that had led to their divorce.

Did Nick want children? Sammy wasn't brave enough to ask—because she knew this might be the deal-breaker for their relationship. If he wanted kids and she couldn't give them to him, what then?

Sammy was still damp by the time they got back to his sister's house.

'I can't make you sit around in wet clothes,' Nick said. 'Look, you're about the same size as Mandy. I can go and get something for you to change into. She won't mind.'

Sammy went cold—supposing he brought down a skirt? Something that would show him her scar? That wasn't the way she wanted to tell him. And she wished she'd been brave enough to tell him before. 'No, it's fine,' she said with a smile. 'I'll soon dry out in the back garden.' She indicated the patio table and chairs. 'Do you have a pack of cards?'

'We do,' Xander said, and went to fetch them while Nick organised drinks.

Sammy shuffled the cards. 'This was my favourite card game when I was your age. It's called Cheat—you go round in turn and put down the next named card. So if I start with an ace, Xander would put down a two, Nick would put down a three, and Ned would put down a four.'

Ned frowned. 'But that doesn't sound like fun.'

'Oh, yes, it is,' she said. 'Because you put the cards face down on the table, and nobody knows if I've put down say four aces, or four completely different cards.'

'So if you put down three fives and I don't have any sixes, I put down a card and pretend it's a six?' Xander asked.

'Exactly. And if I've got four sixes, I know you haven't put down a six, so I'd say Cheat and you'd have to pick up all the cards on the table. But if I've got three sixes and some-one else has got one six, we won't know if you're cheating or not…unless you giggle and give yourself away.' She smiled. 'Uncle Nick should be good at this. He'll be able to see if people aren't telling the truth.'

He did. And Sammy let him win the first round.

And then she played the way she had with her family, half a lifetime ago. As a total card sharp. With a grin, she put down her last cards, saying, 'Three fours.'

Nick frowned. 'Hang on, you laid down three fours last time it was fours—and there aren't seven fours in a pack of cards.' He pointed a finger at her. 'Cheat!'

She turned over the last three cards, one by one. The four of diamonds, the four of clubs and the four of hearts.

'But—how?' Nick asked plaintively.

She laughed. 'Because I cheated massively last time and you didn't spot it.'

'You're really good at this,' Xander said admiringly.

She winked at him. 'My dad taught me how to play when I was Ned's age—and I have two big brothers and a big sister, so I had to learn to be really good at this or they'd sit on me.'

'Really sit on you?' Ned's eyes went wide.

She laughed. 'No, not *really*, but when you're the littlest it's hard to come last all the time, and I always knew if they were being kind and let me win.'

'I don't like it when Xander lets me win,' Ned confided in a whisper.

She ruffled his hair. 'Then, young Spider-man, let me give you some tips…'

Mandy came back just before tea time.

'Thank you so much,' she said to Sammy, shaking her hand. 'I feel so guilty about dumping my parental responsibilities on Nick and on you, especially as I hadn't even met you!'

'Not at all,' Sammy said firmly. 'Apart from the fact that it's your birthday weekend, I had a really good afternoon and your boys are lovely. And it's tough being a single mum. Having a break means you're refreshed and can enjoy the kids more.'

Mandy blinked. 'Wow, that's… I'm not used to people being that understanding.'

Sammy smiled. 'Remember, I'm a photographer. I've met an awful lot of people and heard an awful lot of life stories over the years.' She blew on her nails and polished them against her T-shirt. 'Very wise that makes me, young Padawan.'

Mandy laughed. 'If you're Yoda, then how old does that make me?'

Sammy laughed back. 'About the same age as my oldest brother, I'd guess. Which is—ooh—*ancient*.'

Mandy grinned. 'I like you. Would you stay and have dinner with us?' She wrinkled her nose. 'Though I guess you'd want to spend some time alone with Nick.'

'If you're offering me just about anything followed by birthday cake that isn't chocolate,' Sammy said, 'I'm all yours. *And* I'll do the washing up.'

'Deal, even though I'd always pick chocolate cake first,' Mandy said with another grin. 'I take back what I said. I *really* like you.'

Sammy smiled. 'If you're like your brother and your sons, then I like you, too.'

'I like your hair—it's a pretty radical cut, but you've got the bone structure to get away with it.'

'Thank you,' Sammy said, 'but I don't have it cut this short for fashion.'

'What, then?'

'Didn't Nick tell you? I grow my hair and donate it every two years, when it's long enough to make a child's wig,' Sammy explained.

'A kid who's had chemo?' Mandy swallowed hard. 'Xander lost his hair when he had chemo.'

'That's the downside of chemo—but he's doing just fine,' Sammy said softly. 'Thanks to you, he's really well adjusted.'

'I hope so.'

Sammy saw the sheen of tears in Mandy's eyes and hugged her. 'Sorry, I didn't mean to make you cry.'

'It's not you—it just catches me unawares sometimes. I never met anyone who donated hair before. Maybe that's something I can do in the future,' Mandy said thoughtfully.

'My sister's a teacher. She makes everyone in the staff room sponsor her before we have our hair cut,' Sammy said.

Mandy nodded. 'I could do that, too.'

'And if you don't want to do it on your own, join us—except it's going to be another two years before our hair's long enough to do it again.'

'I'll do it next week,' Mandy said. 'And then I'll join you in two years.'

'It's a deal,' Sammy said.

She enjoyed sharing pizza, garlic bread and birthday cake with Nick's family. Later that evening, Nick took her home. 'Thank you,' he said as they sat in the car outside her flat. 'You've been brilliant.'

'I had a great day,' she said. 'I loved the zip-wire. And the water fight.'

His eyes went hot. 'Yeah. Me, too.'

She kissed him. 'You have no idea how many of the mums were ogling you.'

'You have no idea how many of the dads were ogling *you*,' he countered. 'You're a natural with kids.' He paused. 'I probably shouldn't ask you this, but would you think about having your own, some day?'

'Maybe,' she said carefully. And this really was the crunch question, as far as she was concerned. Now he'd brought it up, she'd have to be brave and ask him. 'What about you?'

'Some day.' He looked sad. 'I wanted them about five years ago, but my ex wasn't keen.'

'Is that why you broke up with her?' She realised how bad that sounded and clapped her hand to her mouth. 'Sorry. I was being intrusive. You don't have to answer that.'

'No, that's fine. And no, it isn't why we broke up. You could say that my job got in the way.'

From the look on his face, Sammy was pretty sure there was more to it than that, but now wasn't the time to pry. 'I'm sorry,' she said again.

'It wasn't your fault, so there's no need to apologise.' He leaned forward and stole a kiss. 'But every cloud has a silver lining. It means that you and I got to meet.'

'There is that to it.' But he definitely wanted kids, and she might not be able to do that. She needed time to think. Time to work out how to tell him the truth about herself. She kissed him lingeringly. 'I would invite you in, but—'

'—you've got an early start tomorrow?' he guessed. 'Even on a Sunday?'

'That's the thing about being a freelance—you never really know what hours you're going to work from week to week,' she said lightly.

'Yeah. Call me later,' he said softly, 'and

maybe we can do something when we're both free.'

'Great idea.' She stroked his face. 'Thank you for letting me share today with you.'

'My pleasure.'

Mandy called Nick later that evening. 'I really like her, and so do the boys. They haven't stopped talking about her since she left.'

'Uh-huh,' Nick said, knowing that there was going to be more.

'She's a million miles away from Naomi—that one would never have had a water fight with the boys.'

No. Naomi had never really taken to them. 'Or ganged up on me so blatantly,' he said. 'You know the three of them soaked me in the park?'

'Suck it up and deal with it, you big baby,' Mandy said, laughing. 'But, seriously, Nick, Xander thinks she's amazing. She had a chat with him in the park—he wouldn't tell me what she said, but his attitude's changed. He said he wasn't going to let cancer define him.'

'Sammy's sister had cancer,' he said.

'The one who donates her hair for wigs, too?'

'Yes,' he said.

'And I bet Sammy was there for her every

step of the way.' She paused. 'Nick, I know how you feel about relationships, but I'm telling you now that Sammy's different. She's a keeper.'

Yeah, he knew.

But sometimes he thought he could see something in Sammy's eyes—something she was holding back. He really wasn't sure if she felt the same way about him that he was starting to feel about her.

Did he have the spirit to risk his heart again?

And, knowing that relationships weren't his strong point, was it fair to her?

CHAPTER NINE

LATER IN THE WEEK, Sammy had a girly pizza night with Claire, Ashleigh and her sister Jenny. She ended up telling them about the interview she'd given Ben. And admitting that she'd met Nick's family.

'Have you told Nick about your leg, yet?' Claire asked.

'I've tried telling him a few times,' Sammy said miserably. 'But I keep chickening out at the last minute. And what if he reacts badly when he realises I've kept it from him all this time—especially as I've had loads of chances to tell him the truth?'

'He might be a bit upset at first that you kept it from him,' Jenny said, 'but then he'll think about it and realise that it's a hell of a thing to tell someone. And then it will be fine.'

'Hmm.' Sammy wasn't so sure.

'Give him a chance, Sammy,' Ashleigh urged. 'Tell him.'

'I'll do it when I get back from New York next week, I promise,' Sammy said.

And she really meant to do it.

Except, when she got back to the airport, Nick was waiting for her right by the arrivals gate. Seeing him so unexpectedly totally threw her.

He took her suitcase and the heaviest of her photographic boxes from her. 'How was your flight?'

'Fine.' She frowned. 'Hang on, what are you doing here?'

'The trial finished at lunchtime and I had some time to kill. I thought you might like a lift home.'

She knew part of that was a fib—following one trial, Nick would be in the middle of doing prep work for the next one, so he'd clearly taken time off just to meet her here—but it was so good to see him.

'Did you eat on the plane?' he asked.

'I had a sandwich, so I'm fine.'

He gave her a sidelong look. 'I've never seen you in a business suit before.'

'I'm not always a complete scruff,' she said. And she was very glad that she was wearing thick opaque tights, to hide her scars and avoid any awkward questions.

'No, I didn't mean that,' he said. 'I'm just used to you wearing black trousers. Smart ones.' He stopped and kissed her. 'You look fabulous. And I've missed you.'

'I've missed you, too,' she admitted, kissing him back.

He loaded her luggage into his car and drove her back to her flat.

'Do you want to come in for a coffee?' she asked.

'I'd love to.'

Her heart hammered. She was going to tell him now. Give him the choice to walk away, the way Bryn and the others had, or to accept her for who she was.

She slid her jacket off and hung it over the back of a chair, switched the kettle on and practised the words in her head. *There's something I need to tell you. Nothing to worry about. Just so you know, nearly half a lifetime ago I had osteosarcoma, but I'm absolutely fine now.*

But when Nick had put the visitor parking permit inside his windscreen, he walked back into her kitchen and kissed her stupid, and all the words flew out of her head.

She kissed him back, loving the way his mouth teased hers, warm and coaxing and sexy as hell.

'You make me feel light-headed,' she whispered.

'That's how you make me feel, too.' He drew her closer. 'Sammy. I know this is soon, I know it's crazy, but I've never felt a connection like this before. Not even with…' He shook his head, clearly not wanting to talk about his ex. 'This is ridiculous. In court, I'm articulate and I'm never stuck for what to say. Right here, right now, I'm making a total mess of this.' He brushed his mouth over hers. 'What I'm trying to say is, I want you. I really, *really* want you. And right now there's nothing more I'd like than to carry you to your bed.'

The smouldering heat in his eyes knocked every bit of common sense out of her brain. She'd never been looked at with such desire before. The feeling was heady, and she gave in to her body's urging. How could she possibly resist? She couldn't think about anything else other than what he'd just said and how much she wanted that to happen, too. 'Then what are you waiting for?' she asked, sounding a little hoarse.

He gave her the most sensual smile she'd ever seen, scooped her up and carried her to her bedroom.

When he set Sammy down on her feet next to the bed, her heart felt as if it were hammering so hard against her ribs that the whole world could hear it.

'Curtains,' she whispered. She switched on her bedside lamp, closed the curtains and walked back to him.

'I'm all yours,' he said softly. 'Do what you will with me.'

Need throbbed through her. She'd never wanted anyone so badly in her entire life. With shaking hands, she removed his tie, then slowly unbuttoned his collar. And then she dealt with each button on his shirt in turn.

He really was beautiful. And she couldn't resist skimming her fingertips over his pectorals and down to his abs.

'When I was photographing you for the calendar,' she said, 'I really wanted to photograph you for myself.'

'Oh?' He looked interested.

'In a green glade somewhere,' she continued.

'Wearing what?' he asked.

She grinned. 'The same as any other Greek statue.'

He raised an eyebrow. 'Just a fig leaf?'

She laughed. 'No fig leaf. You have beautiful musculature.'

He frowned. 'Are you telling me you're seeing me as a life model?'

'Right now, no.' Her voice went husky. 'I'm seeing you as my lover.'

'Good.' He stole a kiss. 'I'm looking forward to learning what you like. What makes you smile. What makes you see stars.'

'I like the sound of that,' she said.

He kissed her, then undid her own white shirt, exploring and touching and teasing as he uncovered her skin. He traced the lacy edge of her bra. 'I like this,' he whispered.

'Good.' She unbuckled his belt, her hands shaking as she undid the button of his trousers; she slid the zip down and helped him ease his trousers off.

He kicked off his shoes and got rid of his socks, then kissed her again. 'I think we're a little mismatched here, Ms Thompson.'

Sammy spread her hands in invitation. 'All yours.' She smiled. 'What's the phrase you used? "Do what you will with me."'

The heat in his eyes took her breath away.

He unzipped her lined skirt and let it fall to the floor next to his trousers.

And then, as he started to roll the waistband of her tights downwards, her common sense came back.

It felt as if someone had tipped a whole bucket of ice-cold water over her.

She couldn't do this.

Not now.

Maybe not ever.

Memories echoed in her head. The disgust in her last boyfriend's eyes when he'd seen her leg. The way Bryn had always insisted on having the light off, as if he couldn't bear to see her skin. He'd said it was because he hadn't been able to bear to think about her being in pain, but she'd known the truth. Her scar had repulsed him.

She knew Nick wasn't Bryn. In her head, she knew he was a good man. That he'd understand.

But the fear was too strong. She really, really couldn't do this.

'Sammy?' Nick stopped, clearly seeing that she was upset.

She shook her head. 'I can't do this. I'm sorry. I thought I could. But I can't.'

'What's wrong?' He curled his fingers round hers. 'Tell me.'

That was the point. She couldn't. Every single time she tried, her throat felt as if it had filled with sand. And she sure as hell wasn't going to show him. Apart from being unfair to him—it would come as a total shock—she couldn't bear to see the disgust or the pity in his face when he saw her leg.

Right now, she felt totally inadequate. She'd so wanted to do this. She'd so wanted to be *normal* and to make love with the most gorgeous man she'd ever met. But she wasn't normal, she never would be, and she knew she could never have the uncomplicated relationship she'd longed for.

And the panic flooding through her was far, far stronger than the voice of reason.

'I can't do this, Nick.' Her breath hitched. 'You have to go.'

He shook his head, his dark eyes filled with concern. 'Sammy, I can't just leave you on your own when you're upset.'

'Please, Nick. Just go.' She dropped her gaze. 'It's not you. Nothing you've done. It's me.' She was too scared to face the fear, too pathetic and weak and snivelling. She pulled her hand away from his and crossed her arms over her breasts.

'Sammy?'

'Please, just go,' she repeated.

She couldn't look at him. But she could hear the puzzlement in his voice, the concern. 'Sammy, you're clearly upset and I'm really not happy about leaving you on your own like this when something's obviously badly wrong. Can I ring someone for you? Your sister? Your friend who made you the dress?'

Why did he have to be so nice about it? Why couldn't he just lose his temper and storm out? Why couldn't he be one of those horrible men she'd dated before?

Holding the tears back took so much effort. 'I can't do this, Nick. I just can't. I can't be with you.' She'd been stupid and selfish to think that this would work. 'This thing between us isn't going to work. It's not you, it's me.'

'But why?'

'It just *is*. I'm sorry. I really wish it could be different.' That at least was true. 'But we can't be together any more. It's over.'

'But—I thought we were getting closer.' His voice was full of hurt. 'You met my family. We…' He stopped.

Yeah. They had been getting closer. She

really liked his family. And they'd just been about to make love.

But this wasn't fair of her. Even if he could cope with her being a cancer survivor, there were the complications. The fertility issues. She knew he wanted kids of his own, and she might not be able to offer him that. She'd been unfair and selfish to let things go this far. She should've stuck to her rules and ended it at the third date. Before either of them got hurt.

'I'm sorry,' she said. 'Please go, Nick.'

Nick dragged his clothes on in silence, too stunned to say any more.

Sammy had ended their relationship.

Just when he thought they were moving closer to the next stage. To making more of a commitment to each other.

They'd almost made love, for pity's sake.

There was clearly something very badly wrong, something that had upset her, but she obviously didn't trust him enough to tell him what it was. Which made him feel like something that had just crawled out from under a stone.

Pain lanced through him. It looked as if he'd made the same mistake all over again. He was pretty sure that, unlike Naomi, Sammy wasn't having an affair and using his workaholic tendencies as an excuse to make him the one at fault for the break-up. But, just as he had last time, he'd invested more of himself in the relationship than his partner had. Sammy had made it clear that she didn't feel the same way about him that he felt about her.

Right now she couldn't even bear to look at him.

Feeling horrible, he left in silence and drove back to his flat. It was an effort to concentrate, and a couple of taxis beeped their horns at him for not driving on the second that the traffic lights had turned green. And he was none the wiser by the time he got home. Why something that had felt so special had just dissolved into nothingness. But he'd just have to suck it up and deal with it. He'd done it before and survived.

He tried calling her the next day. If nothing else, just to be sure that she was OK—because he was pretty sure that he'd seen fear in her face. Something was wrong, he was sure.

But she didn't answer her phone or return his messages.

Just silence.

And he wasn't pathetic enough to keep trying to talk to her when his attentions weren't welcome.

Over the next week and a half, Nick buried himself in work—that, at least, would never let him down. And he stonewalled any questions until people finally stopped asking him if everything was OK.

It wasn't OK.

But it would be.

Eventually.

Sammy's eyes felt three times the size of normal—she'd cried for so long. But she knew from experience that the best way to deal with heartache was to concentrate on her work and not leave even the tiniest moment free for the pain to make itself felt.

Though she had to tell a white lie at her photo shoot, the morning after she'd broken up with Nick. 'I've got conjunctivitis,' she said, 'so I need to wear dark glasses.'

Her eyes were sore and puffy, all right. But from crying, not from an eye infection.

It felt as if she'd made the biggest mistake of her life.

But she knew she'd done the right thing in the long run.

She just hoped it would stop hurting soon.

'I know something's wrong,' Mandy said. 'I'm your big sister. You can't fob me off with any more excuses. And Danica next door is babysitting the boys, so I can stay here until you finally tell me what's wrong.'

Nick sighed. 'OK. Sammy and I have split up.'

'What? But why did you dump her? Sammy was lovely,' Mandy said.

'I didn't dump her. She dumped me.' Nick shrugged.

'No *way*,' Mandy said, sounding shocked. 'The way she was with you—I could see how much she thought of you. You must've got it wrong.'

'She said it wasn't working for her. And you can't force someone to feel something they don't.' He looked away. 'At least I didn't make a total fool out of myself and tell her how I felt about her before she dumped me.'

'Oh, Nick.' Mandy hugged him. 'Are you sure you're not just being a typical bloke and totally misreading things?'

'Pretty sure,' he said dryly. He wasn't going to tell his sister the circumstances. Some things weren't for sharing. 'She was quite clear about it.'

'I'm sorry. I really hoped…'

'Yeah, I know.' So had he. 'Plenty more fish in the sea.'

'Except you're not going to even put out a single line, let alone a net.'

'Hey. I have a great family, a job I love, and friends. I don't need anything more,' Nick said lightly.

And if he told himself that enough times, he'd believe it.

'What do you mean, you've split up? You're telling us he turned out to be another Bryn?' Ashleigh said.

Sammy looked away.

'You *did* tell him about your leg?' Claire asked.

'No.'

'So you dumped him without even talking about it?' Ashleigh asked, her voice filled with disbelief. 'Sammy, are you nuts? You broke your three-dates rule for him. Which means he was special.'

'He is.' Sammy bit her lip. 'It was the right thing to do. Now he's got the chance to find someone without any complications.'

'You mean, you were too much of a coward to give it a chance to work,' Claire said. When Sammy flinched, she continued, 'And yes, Ash and I can tell it to you this straight, because we're your best friends and we love you, and you've just done the most stupid thing *ever*.'

'Talk to him,' Ashleigh urged. 'Tell him you made a mistake. Tell him everything.'

Sammy shook her head. 'It's a bit late for that now.'

'It's never too late,' Claire said. 'Look, you've got the calendar launch next week. He's one of the models, so he's bound to be there. Talk to him then.'

Except Nick wasn't at the launch.

Xander, Ned and Mandy were there, but Mandy gave her a cool look and steered the boys away before they could talk to her.

And Sammy felt like the nastiest woman in the world.

She felt even worse when her phone pinged with a text from Xander.

You're not the Black Widow. You're one of the weasels.

He was absolutely right.

She went home on her own.

And then she cried herself to sleep all over again.

CHAPTER TEN

'TEA?' GARY SMILED broadly at Nick and placed the mug on his desk. 'Oh, and you might like to see this.' He handed over a press cutting. 'It's about your calendar. Which is selling like hot cakes from the clerks' room, I might add. We're getting people from every set of chambers around here coming in to buy them.'

Nick rolled his eyes. 'The next person to ask me if I'll strip off in the middle of their court case is going to get pushed into the nearest puddle.'

'Hey.' Gary punched his arm awkwardly. 'They're only teasing. What you did is pretty awesome. I'm not sure I'd have the guts to do it. Is your nephew doing OK?'

'Yeah, he is. Thanks for asking.'

'Are *you* OK?'

Nick gave his clerk a pointed look. 'I will be, if people will let me get on with my job.'

'Got it, boss.' Gary sketched a wry salute and left Nick's office.

Nick ignored the article for a while. But curiosity eventually won, and he picked it up to look at it.

It was pretty standard stuff: how a group of people connected with the oncology ward had stripped off for a charity calendar to raise money for new equipment and treatment. And it came with a montage of photographs from the calendar—including his own page. Mr December.

He was about to drop the cutting in the bin when something in the last paragraph caught his eye.

About the woman who'd photographed the calendar.

Who was a cancer survivor.

What the hell…?

He sat up, slapped the cutting back on his desk and read it more closely.

When he'd finished, he just stared at the page, stunned. He'd had absolutely no idea that Sammy had had osteosarcoma as a teen.

Why hadn't she told him? Especially when she knew that his nephew had the same condition? Did she really think it made any difference to the way he'd treat her?

The article implied that not everyone in Sammy's past had reacted well to her medical condition. OK, some people were ignorant. But, for pity's sake, she *knew* him. Surely she'd known that he wouldn't react badly? That he would never have pushed her away or made her feel ugly or anything less than beautiful? That for him, beauty was skin deep and that it was who you were rather than what you looked like that mattered?

Nick thought about it.

And then he thought some more.

He remembered that day in the park. He'd asked Sammy afterwards if she wanted children; and he'd told her that he wanted kids of his own.

According to the article, she'd had chemotherapy before and after the surgery. He didn't know that much about the side-effects of cancer treatment on women—thankfully none of the women in his life had been affected by it—but he was pretty sure that it could make having children difficult. A quick bit of research on the internet told him that, yes, fertility could be a problem, depending on whether or not she'd had some eggs frozen before the treatment.

It's not you, it's me.

Her words took on a slightly different meaning now. Maybe she'd ended things between them not because she wasn't interested, but because she thought that having a family would be too complicated, she knew he wanted children, and she didn't want to stand in the way of his dreams. She'd pushed him away, but maybe she'd broken up with him as the ultimate in self-sacrifice rather than actually rejecting him.

She hadn't given him the chance to discuss it with her. But maybe, if she'd been hurt badly before, she found it difficult to trust. As difficult as he did.

Even though part of him was hurt and angry that she hadn't trusted him, a deeper part of him understood why. Maybe he should cut her some slack. Give her a chance to tell him herself.

When his session in court had ended, in the middle of the afternoon, Nick called her. The line went straight through to voicemail: meaning that she was busy, or she was avoiding him. He wasn't sure which. Either way, he'd leave a very clear message, so she'd be left in no doubt. 'Sammy, it's Nick. I saw the article your friend wrote about the calendar. About you. If you don't call me back, I'll come and sit outside your flat until you get home, and I don't care if I have to sit there for a whole month before you turn up. Because we really, really need to talk.'

'Answer it, you chicken,' Sammy told herself when she saw Nick's name on the screen of her mobile phone.

But she didn't quite have the nerve.

She listened to the voicemail he left her, though.

It seemed that Nick wanted to talk to her. And he wasn't planning to take no for an answer.

She dragged in a breath. He'd read the article, so he knew the truth about her now. She had absolutely no idea what was going through his head. But she knew that she owed him an explanation at the very least.

Time to be brave.

She picked up her phone and called him. 'It's Sammy, returning your call,' she said, careful to keep her voice neutral.

'We need to talk, and I'd rather not do this on the phone. Can we meet this evening?' he asked.

Sammy noticed that her hand was actually shaking. 'I—um…'

'A neutral place,' he said softly. 'Remember that place where we had brunch, just off Fleet Street?'

'Yes. I remember.'

'Shall we meet there?'

'OK. What time?'

'Any time after six is good for me.'

'Six, then,' she said. Better to get it over with as soon as possible than to wait and worry herself stupid about it.

'I'll see you there at six.'

The phone went dead. Either he was busy, or he was seriously fed up with her. Or maybe both.

Sammy just about managed to focus on her work for the next couple of hours, and then she headed for the café where they'd met before. Nick was already there—and her heart skipped a beat when he met her gaze.

Seeing him again made her realise just how much she'd missed him.

But she'd messed this up big time.

This was going to be closure, and nothing more, she reminded herself. Don't think that this is fixable. Because it's not. Your role today is to apologise for not telling him, explain, and then walk away. Don't sit there vainly wishing and hoping for things you can't have.

'Thank you for coming,' he said when she reached his table. 'What would you like to drink? Wine? Coffee?'

'Mint tea, please,' she said.

He ordered her a mint tea and himself a coffee.

Something about his message had really bugged her. 'Would you really have sat outside my flat for a whole month?'

'I would've camped on your doorstep,' he said. 'I might not have been very fragrant if you'd kept me waiting for a whole month—but yes, I would've waited.'

For the first time since he'd called her, hope flickered in her heart. So was he saying they still had a chance?

The waiter brought their drinks over before she could ask. And then it wasn't appropriate to say anything. This was a discussion they needed to have in semi-private.

'Why didn't you tell me?' he asked gently when the waiter had gone to look after another table of customers.

'And you've seen the article?' It was a rhetorical question. She already knew he had.

But she couldn't think of what to say, and it was the only thing that came into her head.

'I've read it,' he confirmed. And she could hear the hurt in his voice. 'Why didn't you tell me?'

'I was going to.'

'We almost made love, Sammy,' he said softly, 'and you didn't tell me—but now I know why you never wear a short skirt unless you're also wearing thick opaque tights. Why you asked me to leave, instead of doing what we both really wanted to do.'

'Yes.' And now she felt miserable and stupid. Why hadn't she been brave enough to tell him? They'd both missed out on something that could've been amazing. All because she'd been too scared.

'You told me that your sister was your connection to the ward—that she was the one with cancer.'

She shook her head. 'No. I told you that my sister donated her hair, the same as I do. You just assumed that she was the connection to the ward, not me.'

'You obviously realised that, but you still didn't correct me.'

'And a lie of omission is just as bad as a full-on lie, I guess.' She sighed.

'Why didn't you tell me? That's what I don't understand.'

She shrugged slightly. 'Because I've found that people treat me differently when they know.'

'Xander has the same condition. Did you see me treating him any differently from the way I treat Ned?'

'No. Well, you're a bit more protective with him.'

'Which is only natural.' He glanced at her. 'Did Xander say that to you?'

'I'd rather not answer that.'

Then another thought occurred to him. His sister had said that Xander's attitude to cancer had changed since he'd talked to Sammy. 'Does Xander know about you?'

She nodded. 'I asked him not to tell anyone.'

He frowned. 'I don't get it. Why did you tell him and not me?'

'Because I wanted him to see that there was hope on the other side of the op, and having osteosarcoma didn't mean that he'd end up never being able to do anything again. I wanted him to see that not being able to play football with his mates is just temporary, and having to rest would give him a chance to find other things he likes doing just as much.'

'Mandy says he sees things differently, so obviously we have you to thank for that. I think you're right—he did need to hear something like that from someone who'd been through it,' Nick said, 'but I still don't get why you think *I'd* treat you differently.'

'I know you're not like my exes. Some of them walked away because even the word "cancer" brought them out into a cold sweat.' She paused for a moment. This wasn't something she found easy to talk about, but she knew she owed Nick the full truth now. 'Except Bryn. He was the one I thought was different,' she said softly. 'He was the one who asked me to marry him.'

Nick waited. Clearly he knew that trick too, she thought wryly.

'Two years ago, I had a scare. I found a lump in my breast. Most people my age would've just assumed that it was probably a cyst and not worried themselves stupid from the time they discovered the lump until the time they got the results back, but once you've had osteosarcoma you have a different perspective,' she said. 'Even though I had chemo before and after the surgery, it doesn't mean that they managed to zap every single bad cell. So there's always a chance that the cancer will come back somewhere else in my body. You need to understand that.'

'But you have regular check-ups, yes?'

She nodded. 'They're annual, now. I have my check-up in the morning; then, in the afternoon—if I'm clear—my sister Jenny and I go out for champagne to celebrate. Every other year, we have an appointment afterwards at a salon so we can donate our hair.'

Then he asked the crunch question, his voice so gentle that it made her want to cry. 'And was the lump cancer?'

'No. It was a cyst. I had a scan and the doctor took some fluid out of it, so they could tell me straight away it was benign. Obviously they tested the cells to make absolutely sure. But it went away by itself.'

'That's good—right?' he asked.

She swallowed hard. 'That's when Bryn broke our engagement—as soon as he knew I was OK. He didn't want to be the bad guy who dumped the woman who had cancer.'

Nick raised his eyebrows. 'But it was fine to dump you when he was sure the cancer hadn't come back?'

She nodded. 'He said he couldn't cope with the fear that it would come back in the future.'

Nick said something very pithy, and she flinched.

'It's true,' he said, 'and he wasn't good enough for you. He was one of the weasels and you had a lucky escape.'

'Xander said I was a weasel,' she said miserably.

Nick frowned. 'When?'

'At the calendar launch. And he's right. I hurt you, and I'm sorry.'

'You're not a weasel,' he said. 'And Xander—'

'—was covering your back,' she said. 'Because he loves you and he knew I'd split up with you.'

'I guess.' His frown deepened. 'I'm still trying to get my head round the fact that you think I'd be as weak and selfish as your ex. You know how I feel about Mandy's ex walking out on them when Xander was diagnosed. I'd never, ever do that to anyone I loved.'

'I know—and I panicked. I'm sorry,' she said again. 'I know you're not like them. But I… I tend to push people away when I get scared. My family and my best friends yell at me all the time for being too independent. Claire—the one who made me the dress—

says there's a fine line between being independent and being too stubborn.'

'She has a point,' he said.

She bit her lip. 'I know. I guess…' She sighed. 'The men in my life either run for the hills or they wrap me in cotton wool, and that just makes me more stubborn and more independent. I'm sorry.'

'You're not the only one to blame. I should've pushed you harder and not taken your silence for an answer. I let you walk out of my life because I thought I'd made the same mistake all over again, too,' he said. 'That I felt more for you than you felt for me.'

She frowned. 'But I broke my three-date rule for you. Doesn't that tell you something?'

'What three-date rule?' he asked, looking surprised.

'I never date anyone more than three times. Then I don't have to tell them about my past. I can pretend I'm normal. That I'm a real woman.'

He stared at her as if she'd just grown another head. 'How do you work out that you're not a real woman? Because you look perfectly real to me.'

'That's not what I mean,' she said miserably. 'It's complicated.'

'I'm used to complicated situations in court,' he said softly. 'Try me.'

'Do you have any idea how hard this is to talk about?'

'Having not been through cancer myself, no. But I guess it's as hard as I find talking about my marriage. And I told you about that.'

'That she broke up with you because you're a workaholic.'

He grimaced. 'I guess that's the anodyne version.'

She frowned. 'What's the real version?'

'If I tell you,' he said, 'then you come clean with me. All of it.'

She took a deep breath. 'All of it. OK.' She bit her lip. 'I know I'm being a coward and putting it off, but…you, first?'

He reached over and squeezed her hand. 'You've been through the kind of hell most people can't cope with—and you still smile your way through life, living it to the full. You're no coward, Sammy. But, OK, me first. I thought Naomi liked our lifestyle—I worked hard, so did she, and we had a nice flat and good holidays and a decent standard of living. I knew my dad had made that mistake with my mother, focusing on his job and leaving her to be practically a single parent as well as having her own career, and I'd got to the stage where I'd started wanting a family of my own. So I came home early one night. I intended to take her out somewhere to spoil her, tell her that I was going to cut back a bit on my hours and put her first, and suggest that maybe we could start trying for a baby.'

Everything Sammy wanted.

And something she might not be able to have.

She pushed the thought away and listened to him.

'I heard voices when I got home. I thought maybe Naomi was home early and listening to the radio, or watching something on the TV.' He looked away. 'And then I walked into the bedroom. She wasn't alone.'

His ex had been having an affair?

It must have cut him to the quick.

Especially as he'd said that his mother had had an affair and his parents had split up during his late teens. It must have brought all that misery back, too.

'Her lover did the decent thing and left us to talk. And Naomi told me she'd started seeing him because she was lonely, fed up with waiting for me to come home late from the office, and our marriage was over.' He blew out a breath. 'And yet she'd always encouraged me to work late, to go for every case that would move my career forward. It was only later that I worked out she'd done that to cover her tracks and make it easier for her to see the other guy. But my job was the perfect excuse for me to be the one at fault.'

'That's…' This time Sammy was the one to make a pithy comment.

'Yeah.' He looked away. 'She lied to me.'

She reached across the table to squeeze his hand. 'And I lied to you, too. By omission, but it was still a lie. And I pushed you away without giving you a chance—just like she did.'

He said nothing, clearly not trusting himself to speak.

'I'm sorry I hurt you,' she said. 'It's not that I don't trust you. I know you're a good man, Nick. You're honourable and decent. All I can say in my defence is that I was scared.'

'We've both made bad choices in the past. That doesn't mean we'll make a bad choice this time,' Nick said.

'OK. Let me ask you straight. Can you cope with the fact that I'm in remission, but one day the cancer might come back?'

'Yes.'

'How?' she asked, wanting to believe him but not quite able to.

'Because one day you might be knocked over by a bus, or have a piano dropped on your head, or be struck by lightning,' he said. 'You can't live the rest of your life worrying about something that might not happen. Yes, there's a chance it might come back. But there's also a chance that it might not.'

'You need to be realistic about this,' Sammy said. 'Because there's more of a chance of me getting cancer again than there is of me having a piano dropped on my head. Quite a big chance.'

'It doesn't make any difference to me,' he said. 'In English law, there's the eggshell skull rule. You take your victim as you find them.' He flapped a dismissive hand. 'Well, not that you're my victim, but you get what I mean.'

'Yes.' She smiled.

'And, for the record, I'm not going to wrap you in cotton wool. I remember you telling me not to do that to Xander, and I thought you were speaking about the way people treated your sister.'

'It was the way people treated me,' she said. 'And it drives me nuts.'

'No wrapping in cotton wool, either. So that's the first elephant down,' he said. 'Want to tackle the second? Because I have a feeling that this one's the really big one. The mammoth, you might say.'

'Second?'

'This thing about not being a real woman. I'm hazarding a guess here, but I read up on the side-effects of chemotherapy.'

So he knew?

'You once asked me if I wanted children,' he said, 'and I told you that I did. But when I asked you, you fudged the issue. Is that because you don't want children, or because you don't think you'll be able to have them?'

'I do want children. I had some of my eggs frozen before the first chemo.' She dragged in a breath. 'But there's no guarantee that IVF will work. So I might not be able to have children.'

'There are other ways,' he pointed out. 'If we want children and IVF doesn't work, then we can foster or we can adopt. Or we can just enjoy being an aunt and uncle. I have two and you have four, right? I reckon that makes a five-a-side football team with one in reserve.'

Her eyes filled with tears. 'Would that be

enough for you? Being an uncle and maybe a godfather?'

'If I have you in my life, yes.' His dark eyes held hers, and she knew that he meant it. Truly.

A tear spilled over her lashes and he brushed it away. 'Don't cry. I never want to hurt you, Sammy. And, believe me, as far as I'm concerned you're all woman. I don't get how you can think otherwise. Unless your ex said that—and you already know that the man's worthless and his views aren't worth listening to, yes?'

'I guess.' The wobble in her voice was obvious to her own ears. It was something she found it so hard to get her head around. 'I can't make any promises that this is going to work,' she said, 'but maybe we can start again and see how it goes?'

'Learn to trust. Together. That works for me,' he said.

She took a deep breath. 'OK. Then I think the first thing is…well, not something I want to do in the middle of this café.' A hurdle she should've tried to overcome long, long before. And one that would have to be cleared right now before they could move forward. 'Your place or mine?'

'Mine's nearer,' he said.

'Your place, then. Which Tube station?'

'The Tube changes from here are a bit messy. Actually, it's just as quick to walk—unless you want to get a taxi?' he suggested.

She shook her head. 'Walking's fine.'

He paid the bill, and they walked back to his flat hand in hand. They didn't say much on the way. Sammy grew more and more nervous, the nearer they got to his flat, but she knew she had to do this.

'What would you like to drink?' he asked when he closed his front door behind him.

'I don't want a drink.' She shook her head. 'We need to go to your bedroom.'

He sucked in a breath. 'Sammy?'

'With the curtains closed and the overhead light on full. In fact, every single light in that room on full,' she said. She remembered where his room was; she took his hand and led him there.

He guessed what she was going to do. 'Sammy, you don't have to do this.'

'Oh, but I do,' she said. 'This is the third elephant. The last one. And it's bigger than a mammoth. Getting on for Amphicoelias size, I'd say.'

'Amphicoelias?' He looked mystified.

'You don't know the name of the biggest sauropod ever? And you an uncle of two boys. Tsk. You need to bone up on your dinosaurs.' Her tone was light, but her hands were shaking as she undid the button of her jeans.

'Sammy.' Gently, he put his hands over hers. 'Do you trust me to do this?'

The lump in her throat was so huge that she couldn't speak, just nodded.

Slowly, he undid the zip, drew the denim down over her hips, then knelt down and drew the material down her thighs to her knees.

She flinched.

He leaned back and looked up at her. 'Do you want me to stop?'

She shook her head. 'No.'

'No?' His voice was so gentle. But there was no pity in his eyes. Just empathy. He understood, and he'd let her take this at her pace.

'And yes,' she admitted. This terrified her. The moment when things between them would change. When he'd start to pity her and want to protect her. When he'd see for himself that she wasn't a real woman.

As if he could read her mind, he said, 'It's really not going to make a difference between us. But you're right—I do need to see this for myself. And then I need to prove to you that it won't change a thing.'

She closed her eyes. 'Then do it.'

Gently, he pulled the jeans down to her ankles and helped her step out of each leg.

She still had her eyes closed.

Then she felt him kiss her shin. Her left shin. The scar. All the way from the bottom to the top, his mouth soft yet very sure.

A tear leaked out and slid down her face; she couldn't stop it.

'Sammy,' he said, his voice husky. 'You're so brave and so incredible and so amazing. And this is just one little part of you. The part that makes me proud, because you've been through so much and you haven't let it hold you back.' He pressed another kiss to her scar, then got to his feet; she felt him cup her face with his hands.

'Open your eyes,' he said softly. 'Open your eyes and look into mine.'

It was one of the hardest things she'd ever done. If she looked into his eyes now and saw the slightest jot of pity, then she'd walk away. She'd have regrets, but she'd still walk away, because this was a deal-breaker.

'Do it,' he said.

She held her breath and opened her eyes.

But there was no pity in his gaze, just understanding. And something else she didn't quite dare name, but she really hoped she wasn't wrong about it.

'You're brave and you're beautiful, and I love you,' he said. 'Yes, we'll have a few bumps in the road ahead of us—everyone does—but we'll face them and we'll deal with them as and when we have to. Together.'

'You love me?' she whispered.

'I love you,' he confirmed. 'I think I fell for you the day I met you. The day you bossed me around and made me strip in front of you—and then you made me talk to you until I was comfortable about what I was doing. And you had dinner with me without being fussy about what you ate. And I knew you were straightforward and honest.'

'But I lied to you,' she said.

'No, you just didn't correct me when I made a wrong assumption,' he said, 'and you didn't tell me about the thing that really scared you. And although I admit I was hurt when I found out, I understand now why you kept it from me—and it's not a problem for me any more.'

'Thank you.'

He kissed her lightly. 'We've got a chance, Sammy. Let's take it.'

She stroked his face. 'For me, it was when you let Ned soak you in the water fight. You didn't care about your dignity. You just wanted the boys to have fun.'

He coughed. 'Is that a roundabout way of saying…?'

She blinked. 'I didn't say it already?'

He looked pained. *'Sammy.'*

She smiled. 'I love you, too. Though I'm still scared it's all going to go wrong.'

'We've both been here before and it's gone wrong,' he said, 'but it doesn't mean that it'll be like that this time. Let's give it a go—see if we can help each other learn to trust again.'

'I'd like that.'

'Starting now,' he said.

'With me half-naked and you fully dressed?' she protested.

'I think we've been here before. Or something like that. Except this time I hope you're not going to ask me to leave.'

'We're in your flat. I can hardly ask you to leave.'

'Then tell me you're not going to walk away,' he said. 'Because right now I need to be close to you. I want to make love with you. And I want to prove to you that you're all woman. You're all the woman I'll ever want or need.'

She didn't need a second prompt. She leaned forward, kissed him, and began to undo his shirt.

CHAPTER ELEVEN

Two months later

NICK SET A mug of tea down on the bedside cabinet next to Sammy and placed the Sunday newspapers on the bed next to her.

'Are you quite sure you have to work today?' she asked, patting the pillow next to her invitingly. 'I was thinking we could have a lazy morning in bed, then go and look at the Christmas lights this afternoon. Hot chocolate, mulled wine, Christmas gingerbread, that sort of thing…'

'I definitely have to work, so we need to take a rain check.' He leaned over and kissed her. 'But I'll text you when I'm nearly done and you can come and meet me. We'll eat out tonight—my treat,' he said.

She smiled at him and kissed him back. 'That sounds lovely, but will you be able to get a table anywhere? Most places will be booked up for office Christmas parties.'

He grinned. 'I'm sure I can find something.'

'Trust you, you're Mr December?' she teased.

'Something like that.' His eyes crinkled at the corners. 'I love you.'

'I love you, too. See you later.'

Sammy spent the morning in bed reading the newspaper, had a light lunch and pottered round her flat in the afternoon.

Her phone pinged at three with a message.

Meet me at Temple Church and bring your camera.

Odd, she thought, or maybe Nick had found out that there was some kind of exhibition or a carol concert on today and wanted to make up for the fact that they hadn't been able to do anything Christmassy today. She locked the front door behind her, caught the Tube to Embankment, then headed for Inner Temple on foot.

As the sun set by four o'clock in December, it was starting to get dark by the time she got to the complex of buildings around the church. She couldn't resist pausing by the gas lamps and taking a few shots; she remembered Nick saying that it was like being back in Dickens' time with the streets lit by gaslight, and he was absolutely right. The light was different—much softer. All they needed was a sprinkle of snow and a few actors from a period drama walking around in crinolines or top hats and tailcoats, and the Inns of Court would look just like an old-fashioned Christmas card.

She headed to the church. It looked beautiful, with a Christmas tree scenting the air and the organ playing 'Silent Night'. But if there was a carol concert on today, it couldn't be for a while yet; the place was virtually empty, apart from a couple of stray tourists.

As she walked in, the music changed. Was the organist playing Moonlight Sonata or was she imagining it? Were they even allowed to play secular music on a church organ? she wondered.

And there definitely weren't any signs up about a carol concert today. Sammy looked around the church for Nick, but she couldn't see him. Maybe he'd been caught up with a phone call or something. Well, at least this was a nice place to wait for him. And with beautiful music playing, because it was definitely Beethoven.

When she went to take another look at the Crusader tomb effigies, a church official came over to her.

'Ms Thompson?'

'Yes.' She looked at him in surprise. How had he known her name?

'I believe there's a message for you,' he said.

From Nick? she wondered. But why hadn't Nick just called her mobile phone?

The church official gestured to the effigies and Sammy realised that propped against the little stone dog that had captured her imagination last time was a cream vellum envelope—and her name was written on it in bold black ink. She recognised the handwriting as Nick's.

Why would he leave her a note here? And why next to the little stone dog?

'Thank you,' she said, and opened the envelope. It contained a cream vellum card. On the front, there was a brief message.

Life's short—eat dessert first.

Something she'd said often enough to him. Hmm. So were they meeting somewhere for dessert rather than a full meal? Well, that was fine by her.

She opened the card, and inside there were directions to go to the café where they'd had brunch. The place where they'd talked over all the misunderstandings and agreed to start again.

Maybe he was going to meet her there, then. But it was strange that he'd asked her to come here to the church first.

'Thank you,' she said to the church official.

She also stopped by the organist, because she was starting to suspect something. 'Thank you,' she said quietly. 'The Moonlight Sonata is my favourite piece of music, and I have a feeling that you might have been asked to play it especially for me.'

The organist smiled. 'I was, my dear. And it was my pleasure. I love Beethoven, too.'

Her favourite piece of music, the Crusader tombs and the café where they'd had brunch. What was the connection? Or was Nick doing some kind of treasure trail?

She dropped some money into the church donation box on her way out, and headed to the café, intrigued. What was Nick up to?

Icicle lights were hanging everywhere on shop fronts along the Strand, and she knew that if she peeped in at Somerset House there would be skaters in the ice rink in front of a massive Christmas tree. As she passed the entrance, she could hear 'All I Want For Christmas Is You' belting out, and she could smell hot chocolate.

This was definitely something she needed to take Nick to in the future, she thought. Somewhere they could both play hard, after a day's work.

'Good evening, Ms Thompson,' the waiter said when she walked in to the café.

She wasn't even going to ask how the waiter knew her name. Nick had clearly given directions of some sort. 'Good evening,' she replied.

'Come this way,' the waiter said, and seated her at a small table with a candle in the centre, next to a sparkly reindeer with a red ribbon round its neck, and a miniature Christmas tree decorated with red and gold baubles. Though only one place was set, and there was no sign of Nick.

'Mr Kennedy says to have dessert on him,' the waiter told her.

'Dessert?' So was this going to be a mince pie, or Christmas pudding with brandy sauce? she wondered.

'He was very specific,' the waiter said. And Sammy couldn't help smiling when he brought out a tiny hazelnut waffle, finished with berries and cream, together with a small coffee. Not Christmassy, but just what they'd enjoyed on their first visit here.

'Thank you,' she said, and texted Nick.

The waffle's a very nice touch—but what are you up to?

Wait and see, he replied.

So you *are* up to something...

This time, he didn't reply. OK. If he wanted to be mysterious, she'd let him have his fun. Because this was turning out to be just as fun for her, too—trying to guess what his next move was.

She enjoyed both the waffle and the coffee. When she'd finished, the waiter handed her another cream vellum envelope. This time, she was directed to the National Portrait Gallery, to one of the portraits that Nick had really liked when they'd visited together.

She loved walking through Trafalgar Square; the massive Christmas tree next to the fountain was lit with vertical strands of white lights, and the fountain itself was lit up, the jets spraying higher than usual. The trees in Trafalgar

Square and St Paul's Cathedral were two of her favourites in London, and she had plenty of shots of both in her portfolio—even so, she couldn't resist taking just a couple more.

Almost as soon as she walked into the art gallery and found the painting Nick had specified, one of the curators came over to her. 'Ms Thompson?' he asked.

'Yes.' She smiled, now absolutely sure that Nick had planned some sort of treasure trail for her. Something based on their dates, unless she was missing something.

'I have a note for you,' the curator said.

It was another vellum envelope, although this time the message was written on the back of a postcard of the portrait she'd been directed to rather than on plain cream card. The directions were to the gallery's café, and the message read:

I'm not going to make you climb over the Dome tonight as the sun's already set—but I thought you might like these.

So this trail of his was definitely based on their first few dates, she thought with a smile. Her table in the café was specially reserved for her, set with a single red rose in an exquisite crystal bud vase. After the waiter had seated her at the table, he brought over a glass of champagne and two tiny squares of toast with Welsh rarebit. Just like the afternoon tea they'd had together at the posh hotel.

'Enjoy, ma'am,' he said with a small bow.

'Thank you,' she said, and ate the Welsh rarebit before it went cold, then called Nick.

His phone went straight through to voice-mail.

She sighed and left a message. 'Nick, thank you. It's very nice having a backwards din-ner, complete with champagne, but it would be even nicer if I got to share it with you. Where are you?'

A few seconds later, her phone beeped with a reply. Patience...

So he *was* there. Just not answering her. 'Arrgh,' she said, rolling her eyes, and sipped her champagne.

When she'd finished, a man wearing liv-ery and a peaked cap came over to her. 'Ms Thompson? Please come with me.'

The next stage of Nick's trail, she thought. So wherever she was going next was clearly by car, because this man was definitely dressed as a chauffeur.

Not just a car, she discovered: a limo. Very

shiny, very black, and very swish. Which, she supposed, went perfectly with a chauffeur.

There was another envelope in the car.

I do hope you meant it when you said you're not scared of heights.

Hmm. Nick had already said they weren't going to walk over the Dome tonight, so what did he have in mind?

She had no clue as the car drove along the Victoria Embankment; they were driving in the opposite direction to the London Eye, so he couldn't have meant that. But then the driver turned along London Bridge, and she could see the lights from the bridge, the riverfront buildings and the fairy lights on the trees all reflected in the dark water of the Thames. London by night was beautiful—but she'd always thought that London by night at Christmas was even more magical.

And finally the driver pulled up outside the tallest building in London—the Shard, its very top storeys lit up with the nightly-changing Christmas light show.

Now she understood what he meant about heights.

Hopefully this meant that Nick would be at the top, waiting for her.

The driver opened the door for her and ushered her inside.

She was met at the doorway by someone that she assumed was part of the attraction's PR team. 'Ms Thompson?' the man asked.

'Yes,' she said, wondering quite what was coming next.

To her surprise, he handed her a filled water pistol, together with another of the vellum envelopes. The note said:

Choose your target carefully.

She remembered the day they spent in the park with Nick's nephews and smiled. Was he planning to have another water fight with her?

'This way, please, Ms Thompson.' The man took her to a corridor. Set in the middle was a table, with three photographs set on a small ledge. As a nod to Christmas, all the photographs were decked with a sprig of holly, making her smile. The first photograph was of Nick wearing his full barrister garb; the second was Nick wearing a suit, and the last one was Nick in jeans.

Which one was she supposed to shoot?

This was a tough decision. The barrister garb was linked to the very first day she'd met him, albeit he hadn't worn much of it; the suit was what he wore whenever she met him from work; and he'd worn jeans to the park when she and the boys had ganged up on him and soaked him.

She tried to second-guess him. A barrister would be super-protective—so Nick, knowing how much over-protectiveness drove her crazy, would want her to take that target down…right?

She aimed the water pistol at the photo of Nick in his barrister dress and knocked it over.

There was another small vellum envelope underneath the photograph. She read the message:

Good choice. Now go to the lift.

So she had got it right. That was a relief.

'Um—could you direct me to the lift, please?' she asked.

'Of course, Ms Thompson,' the PR man said.

As soon as the lift doors opened, Sammy saw tasteful Christmas decorations—swathes of beautiful greenery. But there was also a handmade sign bearing a photograph of a pile of fluffy cotton wool balls, with a red X scrawled through it in pen, and she burst out laughing before grabbing her phone and calling Nick.

This time, he actually answered his phone.

'So are you telling me this is a cotton-wool-free zone?' she asked.

He laughed. 'Got it in one.'

'Where are you?'

'Not far now,' he said. 'Pay attention.'

'Yes, m'learned friend.'

He laughed again and hung up.

She wasn't quite sure what he had in mind but she was enjoying this. He'd clearly spent time setting this up and she loved how very personal it was.

The lift stopped halfway up the tower, and the PR man said, 'You need to get out at this floor.'

Nick wasn't at the top?

'OK,' she said.

But just outside the lift was another table. This one had three cards on it.

The first was a gorgeous shot of lightning—one she would've loved to have in her own portfolio. Inside, he'd written:

Chance of being struck by lightning—roughly one in a million.

To her amusement, he'd listed the source so she could look it up and prove it to herself.

The second was a picture of a piano. Inside, he'd written:

Chance of a piano falling on your head—apparently this is an old movie trope and there aren't any actual recorded cases of a piano being dropped onto someone's head.

Trust him to investigate it thoroughly and debunk the myth. She couldn't help smiling.

The third was a picture of a bumpy, lumpy road leading to the brow of a hill. Inside, he'd written:

Chance of having rough times ahead—one hundred per cent, but I'll be there to hold your hand through whatever comes. Without cotton wool. Just as I know you'll be there for me.

There was a huge lump in her throat. He really meant this.

They'd be there for each other, no matter what lay ahead.

'Ms Thompson?' the PR man said. 'We need to go up.'

'Yes.' She smiled at him, swallowed hard and put the cards in her bag.

Another corridor stop: and this one also had cards on the table. A picture of the edge of space.

I can't promise you this right now, but once it's commercially available...

She smiled. She'd so hold him to that one.

A picture of the Northern Lights and polar bears.

Alternative suggestion to the edge of space, from my bucket list.

And finally a picture of a lighthouse.

You said you liked these. You, me, a bottle of champagne and a spa bath on New Year's Eve. How about it?

Sammy grinned. She was totally fine with that. She scooped up the cards and put them in her bag, too.

'Ms Thompson,' the PR man said, gesturing back to the lift.

This time, the lift went straight to the top—and when the doors opened Nick was right there, waiting for her.

'You,' she said, 'are amazing, Mr December.' She walked over to him, wrapped her arms round him and kissed him.

'You're pretty amazing yourself,' he said.

'I can't believe you did all that for me. And what if I'd picked the wrong target with the water pistol?' she asked.

'I had a contingency plan,' he said.

'Which was?'

'I put exactly the same message under all three,' he confessed with a grin.

She laughed. 'Nick, that's cheating.'

'Cheating?' He coughed. 'And who is the queen of a certain card game?'

'Got it.' She smiled at him. 'That treasure trail you made is like everything we've shared together, squished into a single afternoon.'

'And you liked it?'

'I *loved* it,' she said. 'I really appreciate the time and effort you put in to this.'

'Good,' he said, 'because there's something I need to say.'

She went very still. After all this, surely he

hadn't changed his mind? He wasn't going to walk away from her, like Bryn had? 'What?'

'Look down from the viewing platform.' He indicated the edge.

She took his hand and walked over to the area he'd indicated. When she looked down, she saw five words spelled out in fairy lights on the roof of one of the nearby buildings.

Sammy, will you marry me?

'Nick, I…' She could barely get the words out.

He dropped to one knee beside her and took a box from his pocket containing the most beautiful, simple, solitaire diamond. 'I talked to your friend Amy about the kind of design you'd like, so I really hope you like this.'

And now she definitely couldn't speak. The ring was perfect.

'I love you, Sammy Thompson,' he said. 'I want to grow old with you, if we're lucky enough. I want to live with you and make love with you and laugh with you. Life's not always going to be full of sunshine, but I reckon we can weather the storms together. Will you please do me the honour of being my wife?'

Realistic, practical and totally honest. She knew he'd be there for her—just as she'd be there for him. And she too wanted to grow old with him, live with him and make love with him and laugh with him. 'Yes,' she said simply.

He kissed the back of her ring finger, then slid the diamond onto it. 'I'm very glad you said yes.'

'You really thought I might say no?'

'It was a risk,' he said.

'Someone wise told me the risk was one in a million for a lightning strike. Impossibly tiny for a piano falling on your head. And a hundred per cent for life not always going your way in the future—but we have each other,' she said softly.

'We have each other,' he said.

He gestured upwards, and she realised that they were standing right underneath a ball of mistletoe. 'Well, now. A Christmas proposal deserves a proper Christmas kiss, I think,' she said and kissed him lingeringly.

'And now… I promised you dinner.'

He'd said that he'd be able to find them a table, even though most places would be fully booked with Christmas parties. And she couldn't wait to see what he'd arranged. She smiled. 'You've organised dinner up here?'

'Sort of,' he said. 'Come this way, Mrs Kennedy-to-be.'

They went down one floor in the lift, and he led them into a dark room.

'She said yes,' he said into the darkness.

And then the lights came on, what seemed like a thousand party poppers went off along with much shrieking and cheering, and she realised that all their family and friends were there, ready to celebrate their engagement. Nick had clearly set this up and sworn everyone to secrecy, because she hadn't had a clue.

And smack in the middle of a table—right next to a Christmas tree covered in icicle lights and gauzy ribbon and silver baubles—was a really huge, really swish engagement cake.

'Cake first,' Nick said.

He didn't need to say the rest of it. They both already knew.

She smiled at him. 'Always.'

* * * * *

SPECIAL EXCERPT FROM

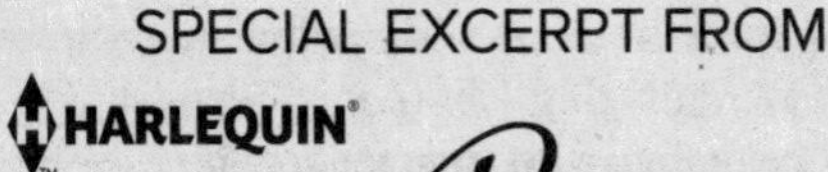

Romance

Will millionaire Jefferson Stone step out of the shadows and sweep Angelica—his new housekeeper—under the mistletoe this Christmas?

Read on for a sneak preview of HOUSEKEEPER UNDER THE MISTLETOE, the sensational Harlequin Romance from Cara Colter this Christmas.

"I'm here about the position you advertised for a housekeeper."

His eyebrows shot up. His gaze swept her. "Oh," he said, "that."

"Yes, that."

He gave her another long look, apparently contemplating her suitability for the position. She tried for her most housekeeperly expression.

"Especially nope to that," he said firmly.

When the door began to whisper shut again, it was pure desperation that made Angie put one foot in to stop it.

The man—good God, was he Heathcliff from *Wuthering Heights*—glanced down at her foot with astonished irritation. And then he gave her a look so icily reserved it should have made her withdraw her foot and touch her forelock immediately. But it did not. Angie held her ground.

She refused to retreat. She couldn't!

After a moment, he sighed again, and again she felt the sensuous heat of his breath whisper across her cheek.

HREXP1015

Then he opened the door wide and leaned the breadth of one of those amazing shoulders against the jamb, the seeming casualness of the stance not fooling her. Every fiber of his being was practically vibrating with displeasure. He folded his arms over the immenseness of his chest, and tilted his head at her, waiting for an explanation for her audacity.

Really, all that icy remoteness should not have made him more attractive. But the impatient frown tugging at the edges of those too-stern lips made her think renegade thoughts of what was beyond the ice, and what it would be like to find out.

These, Angie reminded herself sternly, were crazy thoughts. This man was making her think crazy thoughts. She was a woman who had suffered so completely at the hands of love.

With that kind of track record, it made her thoroughly annoyed with herself for even noticing what the master of the Stone House looked like. And what his voice sounded like. And what he smelled like. And what his breath had felt like grazing the tenderness of her cheek.

If she had a choice, she would have cut and run. But she was desperate. She had absolutely no choice.

With her foot against the door he was too polite to slam, she said, determined, "I need this job."

HREXP1015